"And here i

A rugged man bounded confidently up the stairs. Dog tags hung around his neck. His sandy-brown hair was slightly longer than she thought a military man's would be, and a few curls clung to his neck and temples. He flashed a smile to the crowd and then placed his hands low on his hips and glanced at Piper.

He did a classic double take as his gaze swept down her body and back up again to meet her eyes. She caught the gleam of appreciation and...surprise.

What? He didn't think world-famous lingerie model Piper would spend her day at a charity event? Well, that was why she was here. To clean up her image, right?

Piper stepped forward, offering the trophy to the man. As he took it from her, she leaned in to kiss his cheek, but he turned to face her and her lips touched his. After a split second of surprise he pressed closer, turning the peck into a real kiss.

His lips were gentle, inviting. Her breathing hitched and a heat that had nothing to do with the weather consumed her as his mouth moved over hers.

The audience erupted into applause. Someone whistled shrilly.

Snapped from her daze, Piper pulled away. Her heart was pounding. She touched the back of her hand to her flaming cheek.

Was she getting a fever?

Dear Reader,

When I wrote *Night Maneuvers*, I needed the "perfect guy" for female Navy pilot Alex to date to make Mitch jealous. At that time, I'd just read about the Navy SEAL sniper who had taken out the Somali pirates that had hijacked a US cargo ship. I thought how perfect a decorated hero would be to give Mitch an inferiority complex, and wrote Neil the SEAL as a secondary character. I didn't really think of him as a Blaze hero because he was *so* perfect. Flawed men are way more fun to write. But then, after *Night Maneuvers* was released, I started receiving emails from readers asking for Neil to have his own happy ending, and, of course, readers know best! Neil *did* need his own happy-ever-after.

So, this is Neil's story. Piper is a complicated person and very young. And Neil is so...nice. I was afraid he'd be boring. But Piper is just what Neil needed to shake up his perfect world. I loved researching the South Beach, Miami, setting and learned way more about sailing than I ever thought I would care to, but it was fascinating!

Watch for the last book in this trilogy coming soon, and please check my website, jillianburns.com, for more info and excerpts. Happy reading!

Jillian

Jillian Burns

Fevered Nights

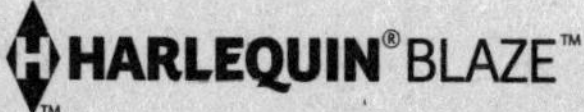

ISBN-13: 978-0-373-79852-0

Fevered Nights

This edition published by arrangement with Harlequin Books S.A.

For questions and comments about the quality of this book, please contact us at CustomerService@Harlequin.com.

Printed in U.S.A.

Jillian Burns fell in love while reading such classics as *Jane Eyre* and *Pride and Prejudice* in her teens and has been reading romance novels ever since. She lives in Texas with her husband of twenty-five years and their three half-grown kids. She likes to think her emotional nature—sometimes referred to as moodiness by those closest to her—has found the perfect outlet in writing stories filled with passion and romance. She believes romance novels have the power to change lives with their message of eternal love and hope.

Books by Jillian Burns

HARLEQUIN BLAZE

Let It Ride
Seduce and Rescue
Primal Calling
By Invitation Only
"Secret Encounter"
Relentless Seduction
Cabin Fever

Uniformly Hot!

Night Maneuvers
Once a Hero

To get the inside scoop on Harlequin Blaze and its talented writers, be sure to check out blazeauthors.com.

All backlist available in ebook format.

Visit the Author Profile page at Harlequin.com for more titles.

To Natalie. You'll always be my "Baby Girl" even if you are all grown up now.

Acknowledgments

Special thanks to sailing expert Joni Dahlstrom of Lynn Creek Marina for all the information about sailing. I appreciated you taking time out of your busy day to answer my questions. I can't wait to go sailing with you!

And, as usual, thank you to my dearest critique partners and plotting helpers, Pam, Linda, Von and Barb. And a huge debt of gratitude to my editor Kathryn Lye.

1

"I DON'T WANT to do this." Waiting behind a backdrop, Piper rebelliously sneaked a peek at the crowd waiting on the terrace of the South Beach Yacht Club. The members of this club were conservative, distinguished. The movers and shakers of Miami.

"Don't worry," Piper's assistant, Ragi Bhagat, reassured. "All you have to do is look beautiful and present the trophy."

Hah. Piper clenched her fists. *Story of my life*. Looking beautiful was all she'd ever been good for. But it paid the bills.

Ragi swept Piper's long hair around to one side and flicked an imaginary piece of fluff off her linen dress. "You'll be fine."

Piper wasn't so sure. The last time she'd been in Miami she'd caused a horrible front-page scandal. Her photo had been splashed on the cover of every tabloid, along with a salacious headline about the "notorious bad girl's" arrest at the cruise terminal. That had only been four months ago.

"Smile." Ragi shoved a three-foot-tall, double-handled gold chalice into her hands.

Piper staggered under its weight, barely righting herself on her four-inch wedge espadrilles. After throwing Ragi a mutinous glare, she pasted on a smile and climbed the stairs to the dais, positioning herself just to the right of the podium with the microphone. The yacht club sat on a hill overlooking the water, but despite the ocean breeze, it was bloody hot for May.

The woman at the podium was wrapping up her speech. "And thanks to everyone who participated in the regatta, we've raised three-hundred-and-seventy-five-thousand dollars for a children's hospital in Miami."

Applause erupted and the woman stepped back, extending her arm to her left. "And here is the winner of the race to receive his trophy, Lieutenant Neil Barrow!"

More applause exploded, even louder and more raucous, as a rugged man bounded confidently up the stairs to shake the woman's hand. His gray Go Navy T-shirt had a triangle of dampness down the front and under each arm. Dog tags hung around his neck. His sandy brown hair was slightly longer than she thought a military man's would be, and a few curls clung to his neck and temples. He flashed a smile to the crowd, and then placed his hands low on his hips and glanced at Piper.

He did a classic double take as he swept his gaze down her body and back up again to meet her eyes. She caught the gleam of appreciation and…surprise.

What? He didn't think lingerie model Piper would spend her day at a charity event? Well, that was why she was here. To clean up her image, right? Though visiting the hospital this morning had been both enlightening and painful. So many children. There'd been that young boy who'd reminded her of Nandan. Her brother had been the same age the last time she'd seen him.

"Piper!" Ragi whispered loudly from behind the backdrop. "Hand him the trophy."

Piper pasted on her most brilliant smile and stepped forward, offering the trophy to the man. As he took it from her, she leaned in to kiss his cheek, but he turned so that her lips touched his. After a split second of shock he pressed closer, switching the peck into a real kiss.

His lips were warm, gentle, inviting. Then they opened to deepen the kiss. Her breathing hitched, and a heat that had nothing to do with the weather consumed her as his mouth took hers.

The audience burst into applause. Someone whistled shrilly.

Snapped from her daze, Piper pulled away. Her heart was pounding. She touched the back of her hand to her flaming cheek. Was she getting a fever?

The lieutenant's eyes twinkled as he lifted his head to focus on her. "Have dinner with me tonight," he whispered.

The bubble popped. Piper sighed. What had she expected? She'd just let him give her a sensational kiss. In public. She brought the arctic to her expression. "I'm busy."

His brows drew together. He seemed taken aback. Obviously he'd expected her to accept. Maybe even skip dinner altogether and jump right into his bed. But that was the old Piper.

He shrugged, then faced the crowd and grinned, lifting the trophy above his head. The applause roared to life. There was a palpable energy rising from the gathering. Bulbs flashed from journalists' cameras, and cell phones were held aloft to video the events.

The naval officer's biceps flexed as he pumped the trophy up and down in a traditional sign of victory. He waved to the people a final time then jogged down the platform steps. No opportunistic speech about his involvement with the charity? Nothing about his commitment to poor, sick children?

The woman emcee reclaimed the microphone and announced the charity race would officially end with the gala ball on the terrace at eight. The crowd dispersed. Piper was scheduled to attend the gala ball. Get her photo taken with the hospital administrator, the mayor and whoever else could help repair her reputation. Must play nice if she wanted her contract with Modelle Cosmetics renewed.

She headed down the steps of the platform and toward the club's lounge. Someone's hand touched her shoulder and she turned.

"Hey, I didn't mean to offend back there," the navy guy said with a lopsided grin. "Just got caught up in the moment."

Offend? A few months ago she'd have already had him in her hotel room by now, going at it hot and heavy. Piper offered him a tight smile in return. "It's fine." She went to leave.

"So give me another chance? I swear I can be a gentleman."

Piper stilled. *Yeah. Sure.* "Look, I know you think that because of what you've read about me I'm—"

"Read about you?" He frowned.

She studied him. "Right. You don't know who I am?"

"Should I? I'm sorry. I'm out of the country a lot."

Out of the country? As if maybe he lived on a ship? Even still. Could he be for real?

"Honestly. I have no agenda but dinner." He lifted one shoulder and smiled. "And maybe a good-night kiss."

His smile jolted through her. She looked into his eyes. Warm brown eyes that reminded her of burnished copper. Eyes that seemed genuine and untroubled.

What would that be like? To spend time with someone who wasn't using her for their own selfish reasons. But that kind of person didn't exist.

Still, she was *so* bored with this whole reformed-bad-girl act. And she absolutely did *not* want to stand around at that gala tonight pretending to make nice. "Okay."

"Really? I mean, great. The club's dining room? Say…an hour?"

Nodding, she turned away, her heart thudding again. Would she never learn to think before she acted? Despite his assertions, the guy probably thought he could get her into bed. Failing that—and he would—he probably wanted his name and picture linked with hers in the papers. His fifteen minutes of fame.

Ragi would be furious that she'd made this date. She'd insist on Piper schmoozing at the gala first. The PR firm had been scrambling to find events where she could make appearances and restore her image. So far, the approach had been working. Just last week Modelle had hinted that they would consider renewing her contract when it expired next month.

She'd signed on as the spokesperson for the makeup company when she was a fresh-faced seventeen-year-old. New on the scene. A rising star in the modeling world. Under the thumb of her agent, Ms. H, Piper's reputation had been unblemished back then.

Now? Well, she'd had a few troubling years. And Modelle insisted their models' characters be above reproach. After Piper's arrest in the cruise terminal, Modelle had threatened no new contracts. Since then, Piper had been conspicuously well behaved.

Yet here she was, back in South Beach. Maybe she should send the naval officer a note, canceling.

"NOW, THAT WAS WALKING, talking trouble right there." Neil's buddy Clay lifted his shot glass toward the platform workmen were disassembling outside.

"The trophy girl?" Neil plunked down on a bar stool and ordered a beer. He glanced through the floor-to-ceiling windows of the yacht club's dining room. The curvy beauty who'd handed him the trophy didn't look like trouble. Regal. Haughty even. Although that could've been the slight British tones in her Indian accent. But there'd been something...fragile about her, as well. And passionate. That kiss had sizzled. "What's up with her? One minute she's kissing me for all she's worth and the next she's freezing me out."

"Well, what'd you expect? Her last boyfriend was a French billionaire."

Neil paused with his beer bottle halfway to his lips. "Why? Who is she?"

Clay's jaw dropped. "You been living under a rock? That's Piper."

Neil gave him a blank look. "Piper who?"

Clay shook his head in disbelief. "She's a famous model. You've never seen her in those Desiree's Desire commercials?" Clay whistled. "And that bikini she wore on the cover of *SportsWorld* last year? She's the most notorious bad girl on the planet."

A lingerie model? Oh, yeah, he could easily picture her in something sexy like that. Neil's body heated. He was going to have to start paying more attention to lingerie.

"She snubbed the Queen of England," Clay said, counting off with his fingers. "Crashed a Lamborghini." Another finger rose. "Dated and then cheated on Hollywood royalty Brad Benton and last but not least was detained by port authorities, returning from Mexico a few months back."

"Whoa, Bellamy, you read all those celebrity rags while you're at the salon having your nails done?"

"You're a real funny guy, Barrow." Clay spoke with the long, lazy drawl only someone raised in the Deep South can own. "I hear all that stuff from my mother. She lives and breathes it."

Neil grinned. It felt good to get Clay Bellamy on the defensive for once. "Your mother's a saint."

Clay's eyes narrowed. "The woman you met is real different from when she raised me."

Neil sipped his beer as he studied the sunset through

the wall of windows. Clay never talked about his childhood in Alabama. Neil could only guess it hadn't been idyllic. But then, whose was? His own mother fell into the same category. She only seemed like a saint to the public.

Though Neil didn't mind donating his time to her charities, he preferred swinging a hammer for Build a Home rather than racing some rich dudes up and down the Miami coast. But at least it helped the children's hospital foundation. One of his mother's high-profile pet projects that looked good on the resume of a senator's wife.

Would he have asked the trophy girl out if he'd known she was a famous model? She was mouthwateringly gorgeous. Creamy caramel-colored skin, delicate cheekbones and full lips. Her long, straight black hair fell almost to her waist. She was tall and slender, but not bone thin like the runway models he'd seen. Her sleeveless pink dress hugged some substantial curves.

But it was her eyes that had captivated him. Neil couldn't get the image of the woman's luminous light green eyes out of his head.

And whether she actually showed tonight or not, he intended to enjoy what was left of his week's leave. Take his mind off Lyndsey and the divorce. Or rather, the almost divorce. Had she signed the papers yet? His attorney had assured him it was just a formality. He was supposed to overnight the final papers to Neil as soon as Lyndsey signed. Neil wanted the whole mess over with.

He tore his gaze away from the purple-and-pink-streaked sky and cleared his throat. "Well, sorry to ditch you, bro, but the lingerie model's meeting me here for dinner in..." He glanced at his watch. "Ten minutes."

"Hmm, what do you know? Straight Arrow Barrow hooking up with bad-girl Piper. This calls for a toast." Clay gestured to the bartender for a refill of his shot glass. "I guess our weekend plans to raise hell are getting off to a good start."

"You're the one who said we'd raise hell down here, not me."

Clay shrugged. "I thought it'd do you some good. You been living like a monk since the separation."

"Didn't know you cared, Bellamy."

That remark earned him a rude gesture. But the idea of veering from the straight and narrow appealed to Neil. And an affair with the hot cover model would be the sweetest cure for the contagion that seemed to have spread in his soul ever since he'd returned from a tour in Afghanistan to find his wife in bed with her lover.

Despite a lifetime spent trying to do the right thing, nearly killing himself to be the best, to make his father proud, all his efforts had come crashing down nine months ago.

Though now he could see that things had been crumbling for years.

Clay thumped the second shot glass upside down on the bar next to the first one. "Least now I can fly back to Little Creek knowing you'll be just fine down here for the rest of your leave."

Neil chuckled. He and Clay had been pals since BUD/S, standing next to each other in lineup, two last names starting with *B*. Surviving the training course in Coronado, freezing their petunias off Hell Week. Going through all that alongside another guy tended to cement a friendship.

Clay clapped his shoulder. “Man, an affair with *the* Piper. Just come up for air every once in a while, okay? You want to be able to walk after your leave is over.”

Neil’s beer slid down the wrong pipe and he choked and coughed while Clay slapped him hard on the back.

“Jeez, Bellamy. You work hard at being crude or does it just come natural? I’m down here for a little R and R, that’s all. I’m going to hire a boat and do some deep-sea fishing, maybe sail down to the Keys…”

Clay raised his brows. “Fine, but this weekend our objective was to find us some women and go wild. And since you’re already mission accomplished, I’m down one wingman tonight.”

“Tomorrow we’ll hit that honky-tonk you wanted to check out. Now get out of here.”

Clay stood and saluted. “Suh, yes, suh!” Then pivoted on his heel and headed for the exit. As Clay took off, in walked the long-legged model in a slinky short black dress that didn’t leave much to the imagination. She’d actually showed.

But now that he knew who the woman was, he couldn’t see the dinner going anywhere. The illustrious Piper probably wouldn’t give him the time of day. He was no Brad Benton. Besides, celebrity models and navy SEALs lived worlds apart, right?

Still, she’d agreed to dinner. So who knew?

When Piper passed Clay, his friend turned around to walk backward, wiggling his brows behind her back.

Neil ignored him. His attention was riveted on Piper. She brushed her long hair behind one ear and gave him a hesitant smile. Neil swallowed.

Oh, he sure hoped she wanted to be bad tonight.

2

PIPER WAS DETERMINED to be good tonight.

But looking into the navy lieutenant's flashing eyes, she had to take a deep breath and let it out slowly. He'd changed into a dark suit with a crisp white dress shirt. But no tie. And he smelled nice. Clean, musky, subtle. "Hi."

"Hi." He pushed away from the bar at her approach, and there was a sense of carefully controlled power in his stance. She guessed the military training must be ingrained in him. He was older than she was. With the crinkles around his eyes, she'd say he was in his early to midthirties.

He nodded toward the dining room. "Would you like to eat here or…?"

"Are you a member?"

"Me? No, I live in Virginia." He smiled. "But I know a guy who is."

She paused. Surprisingly, Ragi had readily approved of Piper's impromptu date, suggesting that she bring the lieutenant to the gala. It seemed he was a decorated

SEAL whose father was a US senator. Being seen on his arm would be worth more than a dozen pictures with the Miami mayor. So her job tonight was to get her name linked with a military hero's.

But to do that, she'd have to mix and mingle and she'd have to use this guy for a photo op. Suddenly Piper found herself longing—just once—to have a normal dinner with a normal guy away from all the craziness of the paparazzi.

Normal. She didn't even know what that meant.

Panic flared momentarily as she realized she'd never been on a regular date. How messed up was that?

What would they talk about? What did one do on a normal date?

She glanced at the white linen that covered the tables, topped with gleaming silverware, flickering candles and fresh flowers. The bank of windows looked out over the sparkling ocean. Soft music played in the background. Now was as good a time as any to find out about a regular date. Ragi would be upset if she skipped the gala. But hadn't she'd earned a night of harmless fun?

She met his gaze. "Here sounds nice."

He offered his bent arm and she slipped her hand around his elbow as he led her to a table by the window. She could feel the hard muscle beneath her fingers, and she liked the way he held her chair as she sat and then scooted it in for her before taking his seat across from her. She wasn't used to being treated so…respectfully.

A waiter handed them menus, and the lieutenant ordered a bottle of wine before she could tell him not to. One glass wouldn't hurt, right? She lowered her menu to meet his gaze as the waiter left. She knew men liked to talk about themselves. No reason this one should be any different. "Do you do a lot of sailing, Lieutenant?"

"Neil." He shrugged. "When I can. I like to sail down to the Keys."

"Those are the islands south of here? Is that really where Jimmy Buffet lives?"

Smiling, he nodded. "Yep, and lots of other celebrities, too. But the best thing is the sunset. You haven't lived until you've seen a sunset in the Keys."

"I'd love to see that."

"Maybe I can take you while we're both in town."

Ah, so he did want to get her into bed. Why was she surprised?

He cleared his throat and she realized she'd waited too long to respond. She smiled. "And did you sail your boat down here from Virginia for the regatta?"

"No, a yacht company sponsored me, so I sailed one of their racers."

"Oh." She nodded and studied her menu. Where was that waiter with the wine?

"My family does own a yacht, but it's moored in DC," he offered.

She glanced up. "And that's where you live?"

"In DC? No, but I'm not far. I standby at Little Creek, Virginia."

"Standby?" She knew nothing about the American military. Or the British one, either, for that matter.

"When we're not deployed or attending a special training school we're waiting around to be deployed. We can be playing pool at this bar called Barney's one minute and the next thing you know we're on a plane headed for an op."

"That sounds a lot like my life in a way. I never know where in the world my next assignment might be."

He chuckled and started to scan his menu.

"What's so funny?"

"Sometimes I never know where in the world I'm going to be, either."

English wasn't her first language, but she caught the play on words and smiled. "I believe *your* assignments are undoubtedly more dangerous, Lieutenant."

He looked up from his menu. "Neil."

She got caught in the warm copper color of his eyes. How could his stare feel so intense and yet convey such warmth? It made her want to squirm and at the same time lean closer. But she did neither. "Neil," she acknowledged with a small smile.

The waiter returned, poured their wine—which Neil accepted without tasting—and took their orders. Piper reached for her glass. Without the menu as a barrier, she felt exposed. Strange. She didn't often feel awkward around men. But then, the men with whom she usually kept company were acutely adept at playing the game. This man…wasn't. And she realized she didn't know what to do with that.

The silence had gone on too long. "What do you do—"

"My buddy says your—" They spoke at the same time.

He nodded at her. "You go."

"What do you do in the navy?"

"Whatever they tell me to do." His sheepish smile softened the sharp answer.

Piper blinked. "And how long have you been doing that?"

"Since I was twenty. Uh, fourteen years, now." His eyes widened. "Wow, saying that out loud makes me sound really old."

"And why did you join the navy?"

"Well, I sure didn't want to be a jarhead."

Piper frowned. "Pardon?"

He winced. "Sorry. It was a joke. Jarheads are marines. We have a bit of a rivalry with the marines. No, it was my uncle. After Korea, the military knew they needed a more unconventional type of soldier for counterinsurgency. My father's older brother was one of the first SEALs. He died in Vietnam."

She raised a skeptical brow. "And this was the reason you wanted to follow in his footsteps?"

Neil's gaze drifted off. "I was alone a lot as a kid. One day I found a trunk in my grandparents' attic with a bunch of old letters. On one of them was a picture of these guys in jungle camo, and a Purple Heart medal. There was also this gold pin of an eagle perched on an anchor, holding Neptune's trident and a pistol in his claws. It's the pin that navy SEALs get after they complete training.

"When I asked my grandfather about it he told me the things had belonged to my uncle Greg. Uncle Greg had written the letters to his parents from Vietnam. I practically memorized them. They taught me the only important things I needed to know in life."

Piper was taken aback at his sincerity, and couldn't have stopped herself from asking the next question if she'd tried. "What are the important things in life?"

His focus shot back to her and he tilted his head. "Honor," he stated with conviction. "Duty." He thrust his chin out. "And love."

Piper blinked, feeling her eyes sting. If she'd ever believed in those things, she'd lost faith in them long ago. After all, she'd failed at all three. Avoiding his searching gaze, she reached for her glass of wine and took a sip. She cleared her throat. Somehow this didn't feel like a normal date. "I guess knowing how to sail well comes in handy in the navy?"

He shrugged. "Knowing how to swim certainly helped. It was about the only thing that got me through BUD/S."

"BUD/S?"

"Basic Underwater Demolition SEAL training."

"Oh. So you blow things up underwater?"

"That's part of the job, I guess. Sometimes."

"Then, I can see why you'd have to be a good swimmer."

A slow smile spread across his face. "Yeah." He nodded. "You do."

She grimaced. "Why do I get the feeling I've said something incredibly stupid?"

"No." He looked alarmed. "I didn't mean to make you feel that way."

"It's all right. You wouldn't be the first." She forced a small smile. "Or the last."

Instead of agreeing with her, he narrowed his eyes

and scrutinized her face. "No one should ever make you feel stupid."

Piper's mouth dropped open. She had no idea what to say to that. This man had only just met her, didn't know her at all, yet he'd touched a raw nerve with such precision and then soothed it in the space of a few seconds.

He took a sip of his wine and the food arrived. Grabbing his knife and fork, he ignored the salad and dug into his steak with gusto. After he'd swallowed a bite, he looked up. "All I meant about the swimming was that unlike my buddy, I was usually last at everything at BUD/S, except for that and diving." He forked another bite of steak and popped it into his mouth.

"I find that hard to believe."

He stopped chewing and met her gaze. She'd been staring at his chest, wondering if it was hairy or smooth. Despite his average height and build, she sensed strength in his every move. Power lurking beneath the surface. Just thinking about the muscles that bunched under his suit coat made her want to slide it off and run her hands down his arms.

Her face heated. She concentrated on her salad, picking at the spinach.

"That really all you're going to eat?"

"If I want to continue to work."

Funny, she wasn't the least bit interested in food right now. Usually, limiting her caloric intake was a struggle. When she'd first arrived in London, she'd wanted to stuff her face every chance she got. But Ms. H had controlled her diet with an iron hand from the beginning.

It had seemed a ridiculous paradox to her at first;

living in such luxury and yet still going hungry. But at least she'd been allowed to send money back to Nandan.

"Doesn't seem right." He shook his head. "Making women think that putting on a few pounds is the end of the world. Most guys I know don't give a rat's…behind about that."

She bristled. "It's my job."

He winced. "I didn't mean—" He sighed and gave her that lopsided grin. "I seem to be having an off night. Usually I'm a lot more suave than this."

When his white teeth flashed and his eyes twinkled like that it was impossible to remain immune to his charm. Besides, it was a reassuring concept. To think that she could quit modeling and eat whatever she wanted, as much as she wanted, and the world would still spin on its axis. Her shoulders sagged. "I shouldn't be so sensitive. Tell me more about BUD/S."

His attention seemed to turn inward and he remained silent.

"You don't want to talk about it?"

"No, that's not it. I'm just not sure any description could do it justice."

"Please, I'm very curious." Genuinely, she wasn't bored at all.

After a brief hesitation, he set down his knife and fork. "Okay." He took a deep breath, braced his elbows on the table and folded his arms one on top of the other. "The first eight weeks is PT. Physical training. Timed runs, obstacle course, timed swims—and we're talking in the Pacific. You get used to being frozen, wet and miserable. And no sleep. The worst is Hell Week.

I don't know how many times I almost quit. Our class started with over two hundred guys, and at the end of the six months, only fourteen graduated."

"Wow."

"Bellamy was always first to finish everything. Push-ups, pull-ups, sit-ups. I'd come straggling in last—or not even finish—and have to do it all over again. Except swimming. Like I said, being good in the water saved me.

"The next eight weeks we still ran the beach, the obstacle or O-course, but we were mainly in the water. Swimming, diving, SCUBA, underwater combat. Holding your breath till you think your lungs will explode."

Piper couldn't imagine. Why would anyone volunteer for such hardship?

"The last nine weeks we learned weapons, demolition, patrolling, rappelling and marksmanship."

"Why put yourself through all that?"

His expression hardened. "My father asked me the same thing. He wanted me to go to law school like him." He shook his head. "I think he had aspirations of me becoming president someday. But there was no way I was going into politics like my old man."

He drew in a breath, sat back and, slowly, his eyes lost their glow of resentment. But his jaw was still set with grim determination. "I wanted that trident pin. Like my uncle. I wanted to make my life count for something."

It occurred to Piper that she was holding her breath. His passion for what he did overwhelmed her. Made her feel horribly insignificant. Neil ensured the safety of millions. She hadn't even been able to save her brother.

He blinked and reached across the table for her hand. "I'm sorry. I've never talked this much about myself in my life."

His fingers heated her, and she curled her hand inward and pulled her fist down into her lap. "I asked you."

"Still, not exactly an appetizing topic." Belying his words, he grabbed up his fork and made short work of finishing his steak and potato. Piper forced a few bites of the salad.

"You don't like the wine?" He finished what was left in his glass and gestured with the stem toward her barely touched one.

She blinked. She'd forgotten about it? "Oh, no, it's very good." She grabbed up the glass and swallowed a mouthful.

He stood. "Let's get out of here." Without waiting for her response, he motioned to the waiter for a check and signed it, then came around to pull her chair out for her.

Before she could think, he'd taken her hand, helped her into one of the cabs waiting outside, and instructed the driver to take them to The Heat Wave.

The nightclub? Deafening music, flowing alcohol, hordes of bodies all moving to the pounding rhythm in dark anonymity. A place like that was like a drug to her. A drug she'd denied herself for months. Oh, to slip onto the dance floor and lose herself in the intoxicating tempo. She could press against Neil's hard body and feel his pulse match up with hers. Maybe the press would follow them, snap some pictures… Maybe that would make up for not being seen at the gala tonight. She could even go home with Neil. Spend the night in his arms. And, at least for now, ease the unspeakable loneliness.

But the counselor in rehab had warned her to stay away from old triggers. To try to rise above doing whatever felt good—but was bad—in the moment. And she needed that contract with Modelle so she could afford the private investigators.

She clutched Neil's arm. "No!"

NEIL STILLED IN SURPRISE. She didn't want to go to a nightclub and dance? He'd almost suggested a walk along the beach and then thought better of it. A beautifully exotic woman like Piper, in her slinky dress and heels, walking in the sand and surf? So he'd figured she'd want to dance. Be around a crowd closer that was familiar to her.

She fell back against the seat and rubbed her forehead. "Look, I'm knackered. Can we just go back to my hotel?"

We? Was she inviting him back to her hotel? Desire for her had been a slow burn inside him all evening, waiting for a spark of hope to show itself. Clay was right. Neil *had* been living like a monk the past six months.

But Neil had pretty much written off the possibility of anything happening with Piper once dinner had started and they'd talked. In some ways, it'd felt like confiding in a close friend. He'd never told anyone about finding his uncle's letters before. Not Lyndsey, not even Clay. Yet he'd also made a couple of colossal blunders.

"Sure. Where're you staying?"

"The Saint-Tropez, please." She answered him and addressed the cabbie at the same time.

The woman was a grenade of contradictions. Her face was a mask of coldness. But her hand trembled. She projected an air of confidence. But she had moments where she seemed unsure of herself and her place in the world. Like now.

She kept her body away from his, leaning toward the opposite window. Though her hand was splayed across the seat and her fingers touched the side of his thigh. She was driving him crazy. He was completely clueless about what she wanted. He'd have to wing it.

Luckily, SEALs were trained to think on their feet.

In no time they pulled up to the Saint-Tropez. Neil paid the cab driver and exited, reaching back to lend Piper his hand. As she stepped elegantly out of the taxi, she was instantly swarmed by clamoring paparazzi. As lightbulbs flashed from all sides, she stiffened. Instinctively, Neil slid a protective arm around her shoulders and pressed her close. But she pulled away and gave a brilliant smile. The crowd shouted her name and stuck cell phones and cameras in her face. Piper posed and looked in the direction her name was called.

Setting his jaw, he shoved through the reporters and propelled her forward, forcing his way through the mob until suddenly they were in the quiet of the hotel lobby.

A few people with cell phones were snapping pictures. He glared at them until they wandered away, then, arm still around her shoulders, he guided her to a secluded sitting area.

Her body was tucked into his, her soft curves flattening against his side. She turned, placed her hands on his chest and looked up. He'd never seen eyes that color. So light a green they were almost silver. And her lips were full and lush. As her lips parted, he caught his breath, lowering his head to kiss her.

At the last second she shifted away, offering her right hand. "Nice to meet you, Neil. Thanks for dinner."

Before he could blink she was heading for the elevators, leaving him alone and…lonely?

"Hey." He bolted after her.

She turned and raised a brow, her face the same mask of coldness it had been earlier.

"Can I see your phone a sec?"

She hesitated, but then retrieved it from her minuscule handbag and held it out.

Neil took it, punched in his cell number and placed it back in her hand. "I'm going to be in town until next weekend. Maybe we could see each other again." Clasping her slender shoulders, he leaned in and kissed her cheek, then walked away.

A half hour later, he claimed a stool next to Clay at the Bay City Bar and Grill.

Clay smirked. "What are *you* doing here?"

Neil shrugged, motioning to the bartender for a beer. "Beats me."

"Unbelievable." Clay shook his head. "Only Straight Arrow Barrow would strike out with a sure thing like Piper."

"Uh, Bellamy. Why are *you* sitting here?"

"Hey, I haven't even started yet." Clay chuckled. "Women."

The bartender handed him a brown longneck and Neil clinked his bottle with Clay's. "Ain't that the truth?" He took a sip, playing back the evening in his mind.

A sure thing? He didn't think so.

Maybe Piper had suddenly become exhausted in the cab. But he doubted it. She'd barely touched her wine, and she'd downright panicked at the suggestion of the nightclub. Only two conclusions could be drawn. Either Piper's antics as a bad girl were purposefully exaggerated—by her publicity team or by the press—or her behavior had undergone a dramatic change. Which was it?

It surprised him how badly he wanted to find out.

3

GO TIME!

Adrenaline pumping, Neil jumped from the helo and fast roped down to the deck of the enemy ship. Pulling his MP-5 over his shoulder, he scanned the area while the rest of his platoon scrambled down. Once everyone landed, they headed below to secure the crew.

Neil darted right, while Deep-dish took the left. Weapon ready, Neil opened the first cabin door and stepped onto...

A white sandy beach. A cool breeze brushed through green palm fronds, and a salty tang hit his nostrils. Seagulls squawked and the surf crashed onto shore. He studied the coastline and spied Piper in the waves, modeling in a hot pink string bikini. She saw him and smiled seductively, wiggling her fingers in greeting.

As if he were watching a film on fast-forward, the tide raced in and the sun set seemingly into the ocean. When the pace slowed to normal, the cameras and her photographer had disappeared. He was alone with

Piper and she was in his arms, pressing her lips to his neck. She called his name and let out a soft sigh. Then his mouth was on hers, giving and taking, until she pulled away, laughing, and ran down to the water's edge. He gave chase.

Catching up to her, he grabbed her around the waist and they fell into the surf, tumbling over each other as they kissed madly. Instantly, he was alone again, lying in the hot desert sand, his arms empty. He looked off to the distance and Iraqi oil fires burned, sending up plumes of black smoke that smothered the sky.

With a groan, Neil woke up, tense, hard and pulsing. He rolled to his back and ran his hands over his face and through his hair. What a dream. Maybe he shouldn't have checked online about Piper before he turned in.

He'd gone down a Piper rabbit hole last night. She was everywhere, he'd discovered, modeling clothes, makeup and jewelry. She'd made the cover of most major magazines and he could see why. The camera loved the exotic quality about her that he'd witnessed firsthand. And those pictures of her in fancy lingerie had literally haunted his dreams.

He threw back the covers and jumped out of the comfortable hotel bed, slipped on his shorts and T-shirt and headed down to the beach. The sun was just peeking above the horizon and the dawn sky was turning the clouds neon orange. His favorite time of day.

Out of habit, he scanned his surroundings, looking for anything out of place. But the beach was mostly deserted. Only two other runners were anywhere close as he hit the sand at a fast jog toward the hotel where he'd dropped Piper off. Yeah, he knew it was a long shot. But a man made his own luck.

Neil couldn't believe how badly he wanted to see her again. He was a simple man. He'd strived for a simple life. Piper was complication personified. And he'd had enough complications lately dealing with the fallout from his disastrous marriage.

That was two failed relationships now: first Alexandra—or Alex—and second Lyndsey. He had to conclude that he was doing something wrong. Some flaw in him he couldn't see. One that involved choosing the wrong mate.

Every SEAL knew the divorce rate in their line of work was higher than average, but he thought he'd chosen carefully when he'd proposed to his childhood friend, literally the girl next door. Clay had warned him about Lyndsey, but then, Clay had vowed never to marry.

Neil scoffed at this train of thought. As if he would, or even could marry a lingerie model. As if she would be interested in a beat-up special-ops guy when she could have any man on the planet. He thought about last night, when she'd sat across from him, asking him about BUD/S. She'd seemed genuinely interested. But it followed that if she knew how to work a crowd, she could certainly work one guy.

She didn't seem the type who normally tried to spare people's feelings. When he'd covered her hand with his, she'd practically yanked it away. But not before he'd felt it tremble beneath his touch.

The shoreline curved and Piper's hotel came into

view. As he approached, he wished he'd asked for her number instead of giving her his. But he'd rolled the dice and she needed to be the one to make the call. *Stop second-guessing yourself, Barrow.*

He came to a halt and peered up at the ten-story art deco hotel. The top two floors were penthouse suites with wraparound balconies. She was probably in one of them. Lifting his shoulder, he used his sleeve to wipe at the sweat dripping down his temple. What had he thought? That she'd be waiting out there like Juliet for his Romeo? She probably wasn't even awake.

Disgusted with himself, he left and headed back the way he'd come. Tonight he'd be Clay's wingman at that honky-tonk joint. Piper wasn't the only woman in Miami.

Even if he couldn't seem to get her out of his head.

Clear your thoughts.

After another mile he finally slipped into the zone, his body on autopilot. Sounds faded except for the rhythmic thud of his feet hitting the packed sand. He concentrated on the air inhaled through his nose and exhaled from his mouth. By the time he returned to his hotel, he'd restored equilibrium.

As he jogged up to the rear entrance, he spied a guy lurking off to the side. Pulling out his hotel key card, Neil kept one eye on the suspicious figure as he took the steps up from the beach.

"Lieutenant Barrow!" The guy jumped forward and stuck a minirecorder in his face. Neil barely stopped the heel of his palm from connecting with the moron's nose. "How long have you and Piper been lovers?"

"What?" Neil stared at the guy in disbelief.

"Were you the reason Piper broke Brad Benton's heart?"

"You people must be hard up for a story." Swiping his key card, he yanked the door open and entered the hotel.

He was stepping out of the shower when three hard knocks rapped on his door. He dried off, wound a towel around his waist and then checked the peephole before opening the door for his friend.

"Seen the morning headlines?" Clay strode in, tossing several tabloids onto the desk.

Neil glanced at the first one. A grainy and unflattering photo of him with Piper as they were getting out of the cab took up the entire top fold of the front page. The caption was ridiculous.

The Hero and the Bad Girl!

He slid the top tabloid aside. The second one was worse. It featured a similar photo, only in this one he had his arm around her as they headed into the hotel.

Troubled Supermodel Shows Off New Lover!

Neil shook his head and continued to read. "Piper's new man is a navy SEAL and son of conservative Senator Barrow from Virginia." Oh, wouldn't his father love that.

A Model of Good Behavior? "Has Piper reformed or is the SEAL taking a walk on the wild side?"

"I think this one's my favorite." With a wink, Clay grabbed up the last one. Neil snatched it from him.

Pipsea! Piper Caught in Steamy Affair With Navy SEAL.

What the— Pipsea? Their names had been shipped? No, wait. It wasn't even his name, but his profession.

Clay sauntered over to the minifridge and pulled out a bottle of water. "So I get to call you Pipsea now?"

"You do and it'll be the last thing you remember."

"You know your old man's gonna have a fit when he sees this, right?"

As if on cue, Neil's cell rang. He checked the ID and then sighed, thumb hovering while he glared at Clay. "What'd you do, conjure him up with some weird voodoo spell?"

Clay looked offended. "Hey, just because my grandmamma was Cajun—"

Neil grinned and clicked Accept. "Barrow."

"Hold for Senator Barrow, please," a woman's voice said, then silence. He almost hung up. But he'd only be put on hold the next time. He clicked Speaker and tossed the phone on the bed while he went into the bathroom to dress, still on hold.

When he emerged, Clay was lounging on the club chair, flipping through the tabloid and munching on a granola bar, also from his fridge.

"You already eat everything from your own room?"

Clay opened his mouth to answer.

"Neil, *what* have you done now?" His father's voice boomed over the phone.

Clay signaled a five-minute warning to go time, and then stepped out to the balcony.

Thankful for the rescue he knew would be coming in five minutes, Neil grabbed his phone and took it off speaker. "Good morning to you, too, sir."

"How could you get your name in the tabloids? If you're going to cheat on your wife, couldn't you at least be discreet?"

"Ex-wife. And you should know better than to believe anything you read in those rags, Dad."

"Whether it's true or not is irrelevant. What matters is public perception."

"The truth doesn't matter? Spoken like a true politician."

"Maybe you can afford to be flippant, but my staff is fielding calls from every major news outlet. And thanks to your impending divorce, my poll numbers are already down. Or did you forget this is an election year?"

Neil never forgot election years. His father never let him.

"Neil? Did you hear me? Drop that Piper tramp and come back to your wife before it's too late."

Tramp? Neil ground his teeth. "Tell Mother I won the yacht race for her charity." He hung up.

PIPER SLEPT LATE.

She'd lain in bed for hours last night thinking about the evening. Was that what a real date was like? At first, it'd been…nice. There'd been no game playing. No hidden agendas. Neil might've tried to take her dancing, but he hadn't turned all macho when she'd ended the night early.

She hugged her pillow and relived the feel of his strong arm around her as he'd tried to shield her from the paparazzi. Another first. Not feeling so…alone. For a few blessed moments she'd let go and let someone else bear the burden.

If she was honest, that was probably why she'd scurried up to her room on her own last night. The energy that had sizzled between her and Neil in the lobby when she'd looked into his eyes? It had frightened her how badly she'd wanted to invite him up to her room. But that would've changed things between them. And not for the better.

A few months ago she wouldn't have thought twice about sleeping with a man like that. But after the nasty incident at the cruise terminal, she'd had an epiphany of sorts. She'd looked back on her behavior the past five years, ever since she'd gotten control of her own money. And she'd been rather ashamed of herself. What would Nandan think of her?

Once she finally had fallen asleep her dreams were of her brother. Always of him. Always a variation of the same nightmare she'd had since landing in London. She and Nandan climbing over the great mountain of rubbish in Delhi—amazing how the stench could smell so real in a dream. Nandan joyously finding a half-eaten roti. They'd shared the flatbread that day. A good day. But the dream always distorted into her searching and searching for Nandan, wandering the streets, calling her brother's name until she woke up crying.

Wiping her eyes, she sat up and padded to the bathroom to splash water on her face. A quick brush of her teeth, then she pulled on her workout clothes and went to the hotel gym for her two-hour regime.

By the time she'd returned, showered and dressed,

Ragi was at the door. Piper let her in, and then sat at the table, her stomach growling.

Ragi was beaming, carrying a stack of newspapers and Piper's protein shake. "It worked!" She dropped the papers onto the table.

"What worked?" Piper took the shake with a grimace. What she wouldn't give for a rasher of bacon and eggs.

"The visit to the children's hospital. And your date with the SEAL. The press has gone wild speculating about your affair. They're saying you must have reformed your bad-girl ways since this hero is dating you."

Piper read one of the headlines. "Oh, no." Her stomach cramped.

"What do you mean, oh, no?" Ragi sat down on the other chair, scrolled through her mobile and then thumbed a short text message to someone before looking up. "This is what we wanted."

"Ragi, this paper says that we're lovers. How is that good?"

Ragi waved away the concern. "As long as they don't have naked pictures of you two together or—" she gave Piper a meaningful glare "—another sex tape, it's all good." She pointed at one newspaper. "This one says that's why you visited the children's hospital, because this guy is a good influence on you. The PR firm is already spinning the story of you dating a navy SEAL. Trust me. Now, what time are you seeing him tonight? I've just scheduled you to visit the veteran's facility this afternoon, isn't that perfect? The press will be there, so be sure to find a navy vet and—"

"No."

"Get your pic—what?"

"Ragi, I won't exploit men and women who've been wounded in the service of their country. I'm not going."

"It's not exploitation. It's bringing attention to their plight."

"And I'm not going to see Neil again."

"But your PR people want you to. This could be better for your career than a dozen charity events." Her assistant acted as if the subject was settled.

"Ragi, it's not fair to use him to fix my career. Besides, I have that lingerie shoot in Sweden next week. I thought we were leaving for the UK tomorrow. Won't the press just label me a callous heartbreaker again?"

"Not fair to him how? He's a senator's son. I'm sure he's accustomed to handling a little publicity. And we can stay in Miami for a few more days. Get some sun, repair your rep here. That's the beauty of having a SEAL for a boyfriend. If he's always away on a secret mission, how can they blame *you* for not being with him?"

"Boyfriend? Ragi, this is barmy."

"Look, I'm only quoting the PR firm you hired, and for now they want you to keep seeing him. I'm sure Lieutenant Barrow will be more than happy to be seen escorting you around town."

Piper made herself drink her shake. Could it be true? Would her appearance at this facility really help raise awareness for injured soldiers? At least the visit to the children's hospital yesterday had been to raise money. And would Neil not mind the horrible headlines? A thought occurred to her. Maybe he'd asked her out for this very reason. To get his name—or his father's—in the papers.

She pictured him sitting across the dinner table from her last evening. Listening to him talk about his training, watching how his jaw had clenched when he told her about earning the gold pin, and the sincerity in his eyes when he'd talked about honor.

No one should ever make you feel stupid.

She glanced over at Ragi. "I would like to see him again…"

"Good." She snatched up Piper's phone and extended it to her. "You said he gave you his number. Call and invite him out tonight."

Piper accepted the phone. "Out where?"

With an I've-got-this-covered grin, Ragi produced two tickets from her leather satchel. "Courtside seats to a Miami basketball game."

4

Neil turned the wheel, tacking the sloop, while Clay adjusted the rigging.

"If only we could've gone through BUD/S in this kind of water, huh?" Clay called over the flapping sails and slapping waves.

Neil huffed. "Yeah, we could've gotten tans instead of frostbite." He grinned as Clay gave him a look that only someone who'd been through BUD/S would understand. They wouldn't trade the experience for anything. It had made them who they were.

However, it didn't stop them from appreciating today's balmy weather. Heading out to open sea, Neil basked in the warmth of the sunshine and the cool spray of salty water. He was leaning over to grab a bottle of water when his phone buzzed. Motioning for Clay to take the wheel, Neil relinquished the helm and then pulled out his cell.

Hav tix to basketball game. Want to go?

"What is it?" Clay asked.

"Piper." Neil sent Clay a smug grin. "She wants to see me tonight."

A slow smile spread over Clay's face. "You dog!"

Neil wasn't sure what to make of the invitation. After those ridiculous headlines, he figured she'd be upset and he'd never hear from her again. On the other hand, maybe any publicity was good publicity for a supermodel. A professional basketball game wasn't exactly low profile.

Neil hit Reply and thumbed, Pick u up at 5.

Within a couple of seconds she texted back, Meet u in lobby.

He shoved his phone into his pocket. "Better catch your big one pronto, bro. And I need a rain check on wingman duty tonight."

Clay looked outraged. "Hey, man! That's not right—"

"Okay." Neil moved toward the bow and started releasing the line. "I'll let the gorgeous model who wants to take me to the playoffs know that I can't go 'cause I have to babysit my poor, pathetic..."

Clay swore. "Fine, but you owe me. I flew all the way down here on my weekend off just so you wouldn't be lonely."

Neil scoffed. "Yeah, 'cause you're selfless like that." Checking the line, he trimmed the jib sail. He and Clay had been assigned to different teams after BUD/S, so they'd never served a mission together, but he knew Bellamy would always have his back. He motioned toward the fishing rods. "Let's catch us a big one."

TURNED OUT THEY didn't catch anything, but they weren't exactly putting much effort into it. Fishing was more of an excuse to relax on the water, to sit back and shoot the breeze. Neil returned to his hotel room with time to shower and dress for dinner.

At Piper's hotel, he'd had to shove past the swarm of paparazzi, but as soon as he strode into the Saint-Tropez's enormous lobby, he scoped her like a sniper honing in on his target. She was standing next to a small woman in a colorful sari. The closer he got to them he could see that Piper's companion was younger than he'd first assumed and that one side of her face was disfigured by a jagged scar.

When Piper's gaze met his, he saw nothing except her light green eyes. She gestured toward the smaller woman. "Lieutenant, may I introduce Ragi Bhagat, my assistant?"

The woman bowed from the waist. "Lieutenant Barrow."

Neil matched her bow and looked up in time to see the approval in her dark brown eyes. Had he passed inspection?

Piper was dressed casually tonight in pressed black jeans and an off-the-shoulder top that revealed burnished dark golden skin. She held up two tickets. "Ragi has secured courtside seats for us."

"Sounds great." He looked at Ragi. "Aren't you coming, Miss Bhagat?"

Her eyes flared in surprise, but she quickly recovered. "I'm not a sports fan."

Piper cut in. "Do you like basketball, Lieutenant?"

"Neil." His attention returned to Piper. She sounded apprehensive about pleasing him, but why? Not for the first time he wondered about her motivation. She could have her pick of handsome celebrity types. So what was she doing with him? He was average looking on a good day. Between training and real ops, his body had been squeezed through the wringer more than once and gotten the scars to prove it. But who was he to look a gift horse in the mouth? "If it's got the word *ball* at the end, I love it. You?"

Piper shrugged. "In the UK, football—or soccer—is very popular."

"You better go, Piper." Her assistant urged her toward Neil.

"Oh, yes." Piper smiled at him.

Neil bowed to the assistant. "Nice to meet you, Ragi." After the woman bowed in return, he accompanied Piper to the hotel's main entrance. "So you live in London?" He'd talked so much about himself last night he hadn't learned anything about her.

"Yes, I have a flat in Eaton Square, but I'm hardly ever there." She stepped outside and headed for a long white limo waiting under the portico. Guess they weren't taking a cab tonight.

As he walked beside her, a dozen media parasites closed in with cameras and microphones, all shouting questions.

"Piper, how did you and Lieutenant Barrow meet?"

"How long have you been lovers?"

"Lieutenant Barrow, how does your father feel about your affair?"

These people were leeches. In the abstract, the fantasy of making headlines was amusing. And really, who cared what a bunch of tabloids printed about him? But being hemmed in as he and Piper tried to get to the limo set off every warning siren. Was this what she went through all the time? Why didn't she have security personnel?

But instead of cursing or shoving the recording devices out of her face, she just flashed that beautiful smile while she clung to his arm. His protective instincts kicked in and he pushed several reporters out of their way. Just as he reached the limo door, another reporter blocked their path.

"Is it true you're pregnant with the SEAL's child?"

Neil froze and Piper's hand on his arm became a death grip. Man, they really did make this stuff up.

But then Piper spun to face the vipers and gave them a playfully scolding look. "You naughty lot." She wagged her finger. "Lieutenant Barrow and I are merely friends." She smiled and ducked inside the limo as the driver opened the door. Neil followed her. Just friends, huh? Why hadn't she flat-out denied the pregnancy?

As soon as they were both in the limo, her scent invaded his senses. Something exotic and full of spices that tightened his gut and made him want to hold her close. He faced her and placed an arm across the back of the seat. "*Are* we merely friends?"

Her gaze flew to his and her eyes flared in surprise. "You're very direct."

He shrugged. "I don't see any reason to beat around the bush."

She gave him a quizzical smile. "You Americans and your idioms."

Leaning toward her, he raised his brows. "You're not answering the question."

Her smile faded and her playful gaze became serious. In the silence he could hear her draw in a ragged breath. His own breathing caught. He stared deeply into her eyes as something passed between them. A frisson of energy that made the hairs on the back of his neck stand up. In the field, that would've been a warning that something was wrong. But with Piper this felt right.

She used her tongue to wet her lips. He stifled a groan. Now all he could see was her full, red mouth. He closed the distance between them, taking her mouth in a searing kiss.

She moaned and he tightened his arms around her, reveling in the feel of her soft curves pressing against him. Just as she had after handing him the trophy, she responded to his kiss, urging him deeper, her tongue playing with his.

After months of coming home to an empty, sterile apartment on base and sleeping alone night after night, he was starved for this woman. That must be why his body was reacting so intensely. His hands couldn't seem to get enough of her. They moved from her hips to her waist, down her spine to cup her bottom.

Giving him hot, wet kisses, she moaned again and straddled his lap. When she rubbed against his erection, his body hard and needing, he almost cried out. He kissed her neck, across her bare shoulder. He wanted to taste her, to possess her. He slid one hand around to palm her breast.

"No." Her voice was strangled, but her hand squeezed his wrist, tugged it away.

Neil blinked as the world cleared from its haze. He tried to get his breathing under control. Embarrassment made his face heat as she slid back to her own side of the limo.

"I'm sorry." He shifted in the seat, his erection outraged at the aborted mission.

What was wrong with him? He'd never felt that out of control with a woman before. Certainly not with his wife. He ran a hand through his hair and forced himself to look at her. "I shouldn't have— Maybe I misread the signals."

"No!" Her gaze flew to his. She put her hand on his arm. "I— You didn't." Her eyes seemed to plead with him to understand. He didn't, but maybe...he did. He covered her hand with his and turned away to look out the window at the bay. They were already on the MacArthur Causeway.

In the awkward silence he heard her stomach rumble. He looked over in time to catch her self-consciously rubbing her midsection.

"I'm starving, too," he said.

She smiled and her shoulders visibly relaxed. "I didn't eat lunch."

"Why?"

She glanced down, running her fingers over the seams of her purse. "I just..." She shrugged. "I was scheduled to appear at a veterans' facility this afternoon." She scoffed. "*Appear*. How condescending that word sounds. As if I was deigning to grace them with my presence. The men and women I visited with are more brave and selfless than I could ever be." She stared at him, unflinching. "Like you."

Brave and selfless? His chest tightened. Good old brave and selfless Straight Arrow Barrow. But he didn't want to be some knight in shining armor, superhero type, guy on a pedestal. He was flesh and blood. With flesh-and-blood needs. He cleared his throat. "I don't know about that, but I could definitely go for a hot dog and some nachos right about now."

"I shouldn't eat that type of thing."

"Oh, yeah." He nodded, smiling. "I forgot. Should we stop somewhere for a salad?"

As she met his gaze, her worried expression slowly turned mutinous. "No."

FORGET HER DIET. The frank's juicy aroma enticed her as soon as they drew up to the snack vendor. She ordered a hot dog with mustard and relish piled on top, chips dripping with gooey cheese and a soda in a cup so large she doubted she could finish the entire thing.

But she did.

It was delicious. It was sinful. Ms. H would've never approved.

But she wasn't under Ms. H's thumb anymore, was she?

Piper licked her lips and smiled at Neil as he cheered for the men bouncing the ball across the court. Despite the flash of photographers' cameras and the red blinking lights of video filming, he seemed to be having a good time.

"I'm sorry about all the press," she said.

"Are you kidding? These are courtside seats. And this is the playoffs."

Whatever that meant. Piper couldn't have cared less about basketball, but she was having a smashing time, too. Neil was a perfect gentleman. If it hadn't been for the tingling of her lips and flutter in her stomach, she might have thought she'd imagined the amazing kiss in the limo.

No, not a kiss. It'd been so much more. She'd felt as if she were engulfed in a powerful force of passion and, oddly, comfort. Wrapped in his arms, surrounded by him, she'd felt as if, for that moment at least, everything would be all right.

"Want some more nachos?" Neil spoke loudly into her ear over the shouting fans and the stomp of athletes' shoes on the court.

She glanced down at her empty plastic tray, and then shook her head. "I can't believe I ate all this." She'd have to begin a liquid diet tomorrow.

"How long are you in town? Are you doing a photo shoot, or just handing out trophies to schmucks like me?"

"I fly to Sweden next week. But I may not fit into the lingerie after all this." She patted her stomach.

After studying her a moment, Neil took the empty tray and cup from her. "Be right back." He got up and disappeared down the corridor beside their floor section.

Had she ruined everything by admitting that? But

what was there to ruin? It was a couple of dates. She was leaving in a few days. So was he.

Then, why did she feel as if she might've just lost something important?

He returned empty-handed a few minutes later, taking his seat beside her and smiling as if she hadn't just admitted to all her bad behavior.

"I thought maybe I'd disgusted you."

He whipped around to stare at her incredulously. "No way." He took her hand and grasped it between both of his. They were such masculine hands. Tanned and rough, with a light dusting of hair on his fingers. So confident. So capable.

"You're what, twenty-five?" he asked.

"Twenty-three."

"Jeez, you're a kid."

"Then, why do I feel so ancient?" She finally looked up at him. Her breath hitched at the intensity of his gaze.

"Hey, I don't know anyone who didn't pull some stupid stunts when they were young. You just had more money and more people watching you than the rest of us."

A lump of emotion tightened her throat. There was that feeling again. Safe. Protected. Everything would be all right. She squeezed his hand.

When everyone jumped to their feet and cheered loudly, he remained seated, his attention on her. "You've done a lot of living in your twenty-three years, huh?"

Had she? In terms of all the things she really wanted to do, she'd barely lived at all. Besides, nothing else mattered until she found her brother. She refused to think Nandan might not be alive. Was he hurting, though? Hungry? Wondering why she didn't come find him? The latest report from her private investigators had turned up nothing new. She couldn't think about what might have happened to Nandan without wanting a drink.

"Hey, you okay?" Neil tucked a strand of her hair behind her ear.

She made herself smile. "Brilliant."

Checking a thick complex-looking silver watch on his left wrist, he stood and then tugged her up. "It's late, Piper. Let's get you home."

Home. Her hotel room wasn't home. But neither was her flat in London. Not yet. Not without her brother. "But the game isn't over. Aren't they going to play off tonight?"

His demeanor lightened and he tipped his head back and laughed. The crinkles around his eyes and brackets by his mouth deepened when he smiled. His straight white teeth dazzled against his tanned face. Laughing. Smiling. He seemed so easygoing, so carefree. So… normal. She wanted that.

Quickly frowning, he swiped a hand over his rugged chin. "What? Did I get mustard somewhere?"

He looked so adorably self-conscious that she giggled and reached up to touch his cheek. "No, you're fine."

He stilled and covered her hand with his. "Come back to my place tonight."

Well, that answered that. After the kiss in the limo, he clearly expected bad-girl Piper to fall right into bed with him.

Cameras flashed. Reporters closed in.

Neil glared at them all. She jerked her hand away, clearing her expression, adopting a cool nonchalance.

Being seen with a navy hero for her career was one thing. Letting herself feel something for him was quite another. And she'd already made a fool of herself over Brad. What was the saying? *Fool me once... Fool me twice...*

Twisting around to grab her bag, she repaired the chink in the armor around her heart. "I think I should just go back to my hotel," she said as she straightened.

The heat left his eyes and he smiled. "Sure."

NEIL COULD TAKE a hint. The lady wasn't interested. He'd like to sweep her off her feet, carry her to her room and make love to her in her bed all night long, but he'd received her message loud and clear.

Still, this time he was determined to walk her to her door. She frowned at him when he stepped into the elevator beside her. He wanted to reassure her, palms up, "Just seeing a lady to her door, that's all."

She blinked at him, that funny look in her eyes again. As if she didn't believe he was for real. He figured the lady had been lied to one too many times. But he could wander around in those light green eyes of hers for days and never care that he was lost. When she focused her attention on him, he couldn't seem to care much about anything else.

As they reached her door, she fidgeted with her key card, avoiding his gaze. "I had a marvelous time tonight,

Neil. Thank you." Her smile was purely for show. What was going on here?

"Piper." He cupped her elbow, laid his other hand gently along her jaw. "Whether you sleep with me or not, I still want to see you again." He inched closer, lowering his head, bringing his lips within millimeters of hers, but he didn't make contact. This time it had to be her decision.

Her lids closed and her mouth touched his. The kiss was combustible. Deep, full of need and something else. A longing. Maybe just for sex, but it felt like more. As if she was asking him for something, but he didn't know what.

He took her face between his palms and angled his head, craving her. As he moved down the column of her throat kissing her, she gave a sigh and then abruptly stepped back.

"Good night, Neil."

Before he could formulate a question, she inserted her key card into the lock and disappeared behind the door.

Neil stood there, his body aching, his mind confused.

Some bad girl she was turning out to be.

But he felt more alive than he had in years.

5

"AND WHAT'S UP these days with everybody's favorite bad girl, Desiree's Desire supermodel Piper?"

Neil froze with a fork full of scrambled eggs midway to his mouth and stared at the fifty-inch television mounted on the wall of the hotel's breakfast room.

Two chirpy morning-show hosts were seated on a bright yellow sofa before the screen switched to a photo of Piper posing in a set of dark red lacy lingerie.

"She's been seen on the arm of a true American hero, a navy SEAL and son of a Virginia senator. Is Piper renouncing her wicked ways?"

"Or," the second host continued as more photos flashed on the screen, "is the senator's son living *la vida loca* down in Miami?" The photos were of Neil and Piper at the basketball game and outside the Saint-Tropez.

Neil shook his head as the hosts blathered on, speculating how long Pipsea had been together, and whether or not Piper was pregnant as the tabloids suggested.

Did these people have nothing better to do?

He had to admit, being famous—or infamous—was kind of a kick; however, he doubted the navy would appreciate one of their operatives receiving such national exposure.

Surprisingly, he couldn't seem to muster up concern. At thirty-four, he was at the tail end of his special-ops days. His body was already showing signs of wear and tear. Sharp pain always jabbed at his knees on his morning jogs. Tendonitis, arthritis, a blown disk. And during his last deployment he'd been more tired, had taken longer to recover. A SEAL in suboptimal condition could be dangerous to a mission. And to his fellow SEALs.

But if he wanted to sit behind a desk he'd have gone into politics with his father. He shuddered just thinking about that.

Maybe he could train newbies in Coronado. Maybe.

"So how bad *was* our bad girl last night?" asked Clay as he took a seat at the table and reached across to snatch a slice of bacon off Neil's plate.

"She's not 'our' girl, good or bad," Neil snapped. At Clay's silent incredulity, he changed the subject. "Where've you been all morning?"

Clay gave him a sly grin. "Let's just say I've been busy and leave it at that."

Pitiful. Bellamy had been here less than forty-eight hours, a stranger in town, and he'd still managed to hook up with someone. Neil, on the other hand…well, he was still Straight Arrow Barrow.

"When's your flight?" Neil checked his watch.

"Leaving in a couple of hours." Clay gestured with his chin at the TV. "So you're going to be a daddy, huh?"

Neil huffed out a laugh. "Yeah, Piper and I are painting the nursery this afternoon." He kept his smile but couldn't ignore the pang in his chest. Painting a nursery. There'd been a time not too long ago when he'd hoped he might be doing exactly that. Before they'd married, he and Lyndsey had discussed having children. He'd told her he wanted three, she'd countered with one and they'd compromised at two.

"Right." Clay grinned and playfully punched Neil's shoulder. "You heard from your commander? Any PR flack?"

"No. But no news is good news, right?"

Clay shrugged. "You going to see Piper again?"

"Listen, all you're going to get from me is name, rank and serial number."

"At ease, sailor." Clay grinned. "Not as if I won't hear about it on the news if you do see her."

Clay got to his feet and Neil scooted back in his chair and stood. "Game of pool at Barney's next week?" He offered his right hand.

"Unless one of us gets deployed." Clay clasped Neil's hand and they grabbed each other's upper arm for a semihug before Clay strode out of the hotel.

As he watched his friend push through the front doors Neil caught sight of a swarm of paparazzi waiting to pounce. He grimaced. Man, if he had to deal with those vultures on a regular basis, he'd crack somebody's skull.

Piper seemed to take it all in stride.

Despite the hype, every instinct told him she wasn't who the world thought she was. Actually, everything he'd witnessed gave him the opposite impression. He'd expected a pretentious, high-maintenance woman, but she'd been completely down to earth. She put on an air of being spoiled and demanding, but he'd seen her reticent and unsure of herself, as well. And she definitely wasn't using him as her latest boy toy. She'd vanished into her room last night as if she couldn't get away from him fast enough.

He probably shouldn't see her again anyway. He was pushing his luck with all this publicity.

Still, there'd been something between them. And the thought of not exploring that bothered him. When would he ever get another chance at an affair with such a gorgeous woman who intrigued him? He got the feeling that if he let this opportunity pass him by he'd regret it for the rest of his life.

Well, no more Mr. Nice Guy. He was done playing it safe when it came to his personal life. Risking everything in his career? No problem. But something held him back when it came to women.

Whatever the reason was, he was tired of being Straight Arrow Barrow. He was the poster boy for nice guys who finished last. Not this trip. He had the phone number of a supermodel. After this week, their lives would never intersect again. Why not try?

He wanted to see how far the heat in her kisses could take him. He wanted to roll around on a mattress with Piper in his arms and hear her sigh his name in pleasure.

With those images in his head, he pulled out his cell and texted her.

Lunch?

While he waited for a reply, he paid the check and headed up to his room to make some calls. But after more than half an hour she still hadn't responded to his text. His earlier determination deflated. Depression landed on his chest like a thousand-pound weight. He slid open the glass door and stepped out onto his balcony. The breeze coming off the ocean made the heat bearable, and he leaned his forearms on the railing. Waves rolled in and crashed to shore. Constant. Relentless. Uncaring of his petty problems.

Then his cell buzzed.

What time?

Adrenaline kicked in. His heart rate sped up and he knew he was grinning like an idiot. He hit Reply.

Pick you up at 1PM

Phase one of the mission completed, he began planning phase two.

PIPER SMILED, PULLED her knees to her chest and hugged them. When she'd stepped out of the shower, she'd noticed the text from Neil.

Neil. She wanted to dance around the room and sing a silly song.

Wait. Hold on a sec. Had she lost her mind? Did she really believe that line about him wanting to see her again whether she slept with him or not? She couldn't help it—simply thinking about him, how she'd felt last night, made her feel…good.

"Ragi, I'm going to lunch," she called out as she jumped off the bed and strode into the living room of the large suite they were sharing.

Ragi sat at the large, expensive dining room table frowning at a manila envelope.

"What is it?" Piper drew closer and peered over Ragi's shoulder. "Is that my contract from Modelle?"

Looking up, Ragi crammed the envelope into her leather satchel. "No, just fan mail."

"Delivered here?" Piper reached for the satchel, but Ragi yanked it out of her grasp.

"The lieutenant is taking you to lunch, maybe?" Ragi asked brightly.

Ragi had never been good at subterfuge. That was one of the many reasons Piper had hired her away from that dodgy investigator's firm in Mumbai. "What is it? What's wrong?"

"Nothing." Ragi stood up, her smile frozen, her eyes blinking rapidly.

"Let me see the envelope, please." Piper extended her hand.

"I'm sure it's noth—"

Piper grabbed Ragi's satchel and pulled out the envelope. *Piper* was written in a weirdly slanted handwriting. No return address. She flipped the envelope over, ripped open one end and slid out a note made with letters cut from magazines and glued to the page.

StAy aWay fROm tHe Navy mAN
yoU don't dESerVe someone LIkE Him
iF You don't yoU WIlL Be soRry

A chill slithered over the back of Piper's neck, and the protein shake she'd had for breakfast churned in her stomach.

She didn't deserve someone like him?

"This doesn't have any postage. That means this guy knows what room I'm in. He could be here, in the hotel." She met Ragi's gaze. "We have to call the police."

"Yes." Ragi nodded. "We will call the authorities." She reached for the note.

Piper studied her friend. "You aren't surprised, Ragi." Her stomach churned more. "This isn't the first one, is it?"

Ragi's silence was her answer.

"How many have notes have there been? How many times has he sent these before?"

"I told you, I'm sure it's nothing. You receive strange fan mail all the time."

"Ragi. How many?"

Ragi blinked again. "This is the second one."

Piper grabbed her cell, but froze with her thumb hovering. "What's the emergency code in America?"

"911. But I've already notified the police. They dusted the first note for prints and ran them against their criminal database. The guy's not very bright or he wouldn't have addressed the envelope in his own hand, but he's not in the system."

Piper dropped into a chair. "So he's not a criminal. It's probably nothing to worry about, then, right?" She wanted to believe that.

"The policewoman recommended we change hotels." Ragi stuffed the letter back into the envelope and the envelope back into her satchel. "And hire security personnel. I've already looked into some agencies."

Piper stared around the suite, feeling uneasy. Having giant bodyguards underfoot 24/7 meant she'd have even less privacy than she did now. But not hiring any personal security might be foolish. How could the creep know what room she was in? She supposed there were only a few fancy suites in this hotel. Staff could be bribed. She should move to a different hotel. No. She should just leave Miami, return to London.

But…Neil.

Even if this crazy blighter was obsessed with her, he was probably harmless so…?

"Don't worry about it." Ragi placed her hand on Piper's shoulder. A rare concession to touching. "I'll arrange for us to move to a new hotel. And we'll hire a bodyguard, just to be safe. Now, what were you saying about lunch?"

Piper let Ragi's attempt at distraction work this time and told her assistant about the lunch date with Neil. She'd make a decision about hiring a bodyguard later.

WHEN PIPER TOOK Neil's hand and stepped out of the taxi, she thought at first he must've given the cabbie the wrong address. The place looked abandoned. When the cab drove away, and she was all alone with Neil, she hesitated. He was leading her down an overgrown path toward a dilapidated concrete structure.

The creepy letter. The deserted location. Could Neil…? She reached in her bag and closed her hand around her pepper spray. But the note had told her to dump the navy man.

Neil stopped and turned. "You look as if you've seen a ghost. Maybe two. Everything all right?"

She studied him. He wore a ball cap and sunglasses with cargo shorts and a plain denim-colored T-shirt that hugged his impressive chest. Over one shoulder he had slung a rucksack that was decorated with a popular comic book hero. And he had on flip-flops. What kind of assailant carried a child's rucksack and wore flip-flops? And there was the concern in his copper-color eyes. Could he be faking that? "What is this place?"

"Miami Marine Stadium. People used to come here to watch power boat races. I remember my granddad taking me when I was a kid. It closed after Hurricane Andrew in '92." He glanced behind him to survey the building, and then looked back at her. "I thought a picnic, a swim, maybe. But I might have underthought this." He winced. "I was trying for a place where we wouldn't get hounded by reporters."

Her doubts vaporized and she pulled her hand from her bag and smiled. He still looked worried.

"I'll call the taxi back," he said, and he got out his cell. "This was obviously a bad idea."

"No!" She laid her hand on his arm and widened her smile. "I—I just had a scare earlier, that's all."

His eyes narrowed and his features hardened. He pulled back instantly to assess her from head to toe. "What kind of scare?"

Ah, there was the naval officer in full force. But she didn't want to talk about it with him. "Can we move into the shade? It's rather hot."

After a brief hesitation, he led her up concrete steps and around the corner into what were essentially covered bleachers facing the bay. Checking for her nod of agreement, he chose a spot close to the water but well in the shade and waited for her to sit before setting down the rucksack and digging out a cold bottle of water. Waves lapped against the shore and a breeze cooled her damp temples.

Neil took off the sunglasses, propped a foot on the bleacher beside her and leaned in, resting his arm on his thigh. "Tell me what's going on."

Piper opened the water he'd handed to her. She'd assumed the topic was forgotten. "Look, I'm sorry. I had a silly moment." She crossed her legs and gave him a smoldering look, placing a hand on his knee. "Don't worry about it."

He took her in with his gaze, starting with her legs and moving up to meet her eyes. She could feel his desire pouring over her. Then it was gone.

He raised a brow and his mouth quirked up on one side. "I live to worry."

Annoyed, she folded her arms in front of her. She'd given him her best performance. It'd never failed with other men. "It's being taken care of. Truly, it's nothing to concern you."

"Piper." He reached out to tuck his fingers under her chin. "I'm already concerned. Tell me."

She huffed. "Fine. It was just a creepy fan letter this morning. That's all."

"What did it say?"

"Neil, I get them from time to time, as you can imagine. It's nothing."

"Then, you shouldn't mind telling me."

"There's not much to tell. Ragi's already contacted the police. It's that—" She sighed.

"What?"

"This time it was hand delivered. Whoever sent it must know what room I'm staying in."

He froze and pierced her with a stare. "When?"

"This morning, I presume. Ragi didn't—"

"And the police are checking into it? What did the note say?"

She shivered, thinking about the message's menacing tone. "The creep glued together cut up magazine letters—how cliché is that?"

Neil didn't smile at her attempt at mockery. "Did he threaten you?"

"Not directly."

"What does that mean?"

Should she mention this part? Though she refused to let some creep dictate how she lived her life, Neil might not want to be involved with her if he knew. He had a right to be informed.

"Hold on, you said, 'this time'? There've been similar notes before this one?"

"Yes." She raised her chin and met his gaze. "This is the second one since I've been here. Whoever this guy is he wants me to quit seeing you."

Neil frowned. "He mentioned me specifically?" He rubbed a hand over his mouth and jaw. "Piper, you need real security. This guy could be dangerous."

"That's what the police said. Ragi is looking into it."

"Good. And you need to switch hotels. Let me ask a buddy of mine about security firms in South Beach." He scowled as he took his cell from his pocket and sent a quick text. "Jeez, you shouldn't have come here with me. For all you know, it could be me sending these letters."

He was angry at her for going to lunch with him? "It's *not* you though, is it?"

"No, but if it were, would I admit it? From now on you don't go anywhere alone. It's too dangerous." He straightened, grabbed the rucksack and extended his hand to her. "Come on. We can't stay here. It's too isolated."

Piper didn't move. Funny, she wasn't a bit scared anymore. She realized she trusted Neil with her safety. "But I'm hungry. And a swim sounds nice. We're already here. What's in the rucksack?"

Neil's jaw tensed again as he stared at her. Spinning on his heel, he scanned the area, eyes focused. "I don't like this. It's not a good defensive position. There's no cover. We're exposed from every direction. And I'm not even armed."

He was assessing their position as if they were in a

battle. She appreciated his concern, but— "Neil, this isn't Afghanistan. It's someone with too much time on his hands."

He spun back to face her, his expression deadly serious. "Maybe. But the guy could also be a dangerous psychopath. I'd rather err on the side of caution." He glanced around the stadium. "I don't know what I was thinking choosing this place. It holds lots of good memories for me, but—" He shook his head. "I suppose we could move up to the top to eat. That way I'd spot anyone coming before they saw us." He looked over at her. "But no swimming."

"We'll see." She stood and started climbing the bleachers. This take-no-prisoners side of Neil was a huge turn-on. She smiled seductively at him over her shoulder. "Maybe I'll change your mind."

6

PIPER'S PLAYFUL SMILE caught Neil right in the chest. Then she had her back to him and her curvy bottom swayed at eye level. She was wearing short shorts that showed off her long, smooth legs. And the royal-blue lace blouse revealed her bra beneath. Only his extreme training allowed him to form coherent sentences around her.

This had to be lust, plain and simple, right? He'd only known the woman a few days. But whenever he was near her, feelings that had nothing to do with lust stirred in his gut. Words popped in his head like *mine.* And *need.* And *protect.* Hearing about those disturbing letters had made him want to lock her away behind an armored fortress.

Even thinking about some other security detail protecting her raised the hairs on the back of his neck. The only person he trusted to guard her was himself. No one else would be as invested in keeping her safe as he was. It wasn't a rational thought, but damn it, it was true.

Once they'd reached the top of the stadium, Neil waited until Piper sat, then took a seat beside her. He dropped the backpack between his spread legs and pulled out the boxes of croissant sandwiches and containers of fresh-cut fruit from the gourmet sandwich shop.

"Oh, this looks yummy." Eyeing him, Piper plucked a chunk of melon from the container and stuck it in her mouth. He watched her lips as she chewed, her throat as she swallowed, taking in her creamy golden skin, the plump swell of her cleavage above the lace top. He hardened. Then he noticed her twinkling eyes. Busted.

She laughed, a dusky, throaty sound. "It's all right, you know. I'd probably be out of work if men weren't totally obsessed with women's breasts."

Well, that was honest. The sophisticated seductress had vanished. She was so young, he realized. He was only thirty-four, but still, he felt old. Was he too old for her? Scratch that. Hadn't he decided no more Mr. Nice Guy?

But she might be in danger. He couldn't take advantage of that. Or could he?

The old Neil wouldn't have. But look where that had gotten him.

Piper's smile had faded, and it occurred to him that his thoughts must be written all over his face. But she didn't seem frightened. Her light green eyes burned with embers he'd like to stir to a blaze.

Her luscious lips parted and her chest rose as she drew in a deep breath. "Neil, I—" Her cell chimed and she jumped. She heaved a large sigh and then found the cell in her purse. She touched the screen, read a text and looked up. "It's Ragi, telling me she's moved us to a new hotel."

"Good. Let her know I have an idea about—" A sound he barely registered jerked him to full alert.

Piper frowned. "What?"

He put a finger to his lips, darted to the edge of the bleachers and sneaked a quick look. A lanky man in a dark T-shirt and blue jeans was sneaking around the overgrown shrubberies beside the walkway. He was holding a camera with a large zoom lens.

Glancing back, Neil motioned for Piper to stay where she was and remain quiet. It was a long way down to the ground. About fifteen feet. Neil swung over the top bleachers, lowered himself, then waited until the guy crept up the walkway next to what was left of the stadium. Neil launched himself, landing hard on top of the guy. They both hit the cracked pavement with a jarring thud.

The man yelled in pain and then cursed.

Neil got to his feet, caught the guy by the front of his shirt and hauled him up. "Who are you? What are you doing here?" He shook the guy until he had his hands up, his head snapped back.

"Are you crazy? Jumping down on me like that. You could've killed me! You just got yourself a lawsuit, buddy."

"After you're arrested for stalking."

"Stalking? Hey, I got rights. Freedom of the press and Piper's a public figure." The guy struggled out of Neil's grasp and bent to grab up the camera. "If you broke this, you're buying me a new one." He fiddled with the lens, then raised it to Neil's face and snapped a picture.

"Oh, *is* it broken? Let me see." Neil snatched the camera out of the moron's hand.

"Hey!" The guy protested as Neil opened the battery compartment, removed the battery and memory card, and then pitched them into the water.

"*Now* it's broken." He handed back the camera. "You send any more threatening letters to Piper and I'll break more than your camera, you got that?"

The guy's face screwed up in confusion. "Huh? What letters?"

Neil analyzed the guy. Either he was a talented actor or he wasn't the author of the letters. Still… Neil leaned in close and got in the guy's face. "Don't come near Piper again." He gave him a menacing glare and the reporter hesitated for only a second before wisely deciding to run.

Taking a deep breath to calm his temper, Neil headed back to Piper, who was now at the bottom of the bleachers holding a can of pepper spray in one curled fist. "Was that him?"

"Not likely. Probably just your run-of-the-mill opportunistic scumbag."

"Are you daft? Neil! You could've been killed!"

He glanced down at her *weapon.* "Were you planning on coming to my rescue?" He gave her a friendly smile to let her know he was impressed rather than sarcastic.

She clicked her tongue, stuffed the can of pepper spray into a pocket and again folded her arms across her chest. "He must've followed the taxi. Just paparazzi, then?"

This time. What if it had been the crazed letter writer? Neil's blood chilled. "Piper." She moved to retrieve the rucksack. He stepped close, clasped her shoulders and turned her to face him. "I want to protect you while you're here."

THE GRIM DETERMINATION glinting in Neil's eyes made Piper shiver.

She knew he wanted her. She'd caught him staring at her breasts. She knew *that* look. But he also made her feel as if she was a good person. He didn't treat her as if she was some empty-headed beauty. When she looked into his gaze she saw genuine respect there.

But he'd just demonstrated he would risk his life to keep her safe. If something happened to him because of her…

She should hire someone else to protect her.

And it wasn't as if he was going to quit the navy and guard her full-time. She'd have to get someone once she got back to London anyway. Or maybe not. Maybe once she wasn't with Neil anymore, the threats would stop. *If* the jerk who wrote the letters was even truly dangerous. She might be worrying for nothing.

For a moment she was paralyzed with indecision. In the end, it boiled down to one thing. No matter how badly she wanted to be with Neil Barrow, the risk wasn't worth it. He didn't need to get mixed up in her manic, unpredictable life. First thing tomorrow she was heading back to London.

But that was tomorrow. "What do you propose?"

He grinned. "I know this guy."

"PULL OVER HERE," Neil ordered the cabbie. He'd directed the taxi driver to take so many turns and double-backs that Piper could've been in another state for all she knew. Admittedly, she couldn't even name all the American states, but still…

Neil paid the cab fare, and then sprung out, reaching back for her hand. As Piper climbed out, she caught a whiff of cumin, chili powder and smoking meat in the humid air. The smells reminded her a little of India. Brightly colored graffiti covered the stucco buildings and the sidewalks teemed with tourists and vendors. Mostly older cars inched along the street.

"Where are we?"

"Welcome to Little Havana." Neil smiled and tugged her to a storefront with a sign written in Spanish. As they entered, the enticing scents made her stomach growl.

"Welcome to Casa Abuelas. Two for dinner, senor?" a young man asked.

Neil swiped off his ball cap and glasses, and then launched into Spanish.

The host's face lit up and he wrapped Neil in a hug. When the kid called to someone in the kitchen, shouts preceded a crowd of people flowing into the dining room to greet Neil, everyone hugging him and speaking rapidly in Spanish.

Neil conversed fluently in return, finally singling out an older man, perhaps the owner of the restaurant.

Neil lowered his voice and gestured toward Piper. The gray-haired man's dark eyes cut to her as he nodded. *"Si! Por supuesto!"* He pointed outside as he spoke and Neil agreed.

"Muchas gracias, mi amigo." Neil hugged the older man and called, "Adios," to them all. Then he returned to Piper and directed her back out to the sidewalk. But before they'd taken three steps, the host shouted out to Neil.

The older man caught up to them and shoved a brown paper bag into Piper's hands. "For you, senorita. *Ropa vieja.*"

Piper returned his smile. "*Gracias*, senor."

He smiled shyly, gave a firm but quick nod of his chin to Neil and retreated inside the restaurant.

The bag was warm and Piper inhaled. "Mmm, smells wonderful."

"*Ropa vieja* is a popular Cuban dish. Have you had it before?"

She shook her head. "I take it you're a regular?"

"Known the family my whole life. My grandparents brought me here as a kid. Their older son, Ramón, served with my uncle." Pain flickered in his eyes before he shook it off. "I'm sorry I didn't introduce you, but the mission here is anonymity."

"It's quite all right. But what was that all about? You didn't come here for the food, did you?" They still had most of their picnic lunch in his rucksack.

"I was asking Senor Perez about secondhand shops. The meal was his idea."

"Secondhand?"

Neil flashed that cheeky grin. "You'll see." Taking her elbow, he weaved through the crowded streets, turning a corner or two. If Piper hadn't been hopelessly lost before, she certainly was now. But she wasn't afraid. Quite the contrary.

Down a tree-lined street, children were playing some sort of game on the sidewalk, chattering and shouting. They were so innocent, so oblivious to all the despicable things this world had to offer. Suddenly Nandan's face swam before her. Playing outside their house, complaining that he was hungry.

She must've slowed her pace. Neil stopped and stared at her.

She smiled at him, but he didn't return the gesture. He merely reached for her hand, clasped it and squeezed. The emotion reached her throat and a prickly sensation burned in her nose and behind her eyes.

He couldn't possibly know about her brother. No one knew except for the private investigators who were looking for him. So why did Neil seem to understand her pain? And his hand felt so comforting wrapped around hers.

She forced herself to bury the sentimentality. It only made her weak. Besides, he probably just thought she was upset about the creepy letter. She pulled her hand away. "Are we headed somewhere or just sightseeing?"

"Ouch." He winked and pretended to wince. "Draw in your claws, we're almost there."

After walking a couple more blocks he read a sign on a store door—also in Spanish—and then pulled her inside.

It looked like a clothing store, but the garments were crammed on the racks, obviously not new. Again, he spoke Spanish to the employee and within minutes Neil was handing her what looked like a maid's uniform, complete with apron. "Try this on."

Piper put her hands on her hips and stepped back. "Seriously?"

"You've moved to a new hotel, right? We go in through the employees' entrance." He shrugged. "People don't notice maids."

Piper heaved a sigh, snatched the dress from him and stalked into the dressing room.

It was two sizes too big, but it was the only one they had, so she left her clothes on underneath and tied the apron tight around her waist. Not a bad disguise, but she still wasn't convinced it would work. She yanked back the dressing room curtain and stepped out. "I think I'll still be recognized."

Neil rubbed his cheek as he studied her, and when his eyes met hers, they smoldered. "What are we going to do with you?"

What would he do with her? Heat built in her belly and spread lower to her core, like a fever. She had to look away.

"Maybe if you put your hair up?" He closed the distance between them and drew his fingers through the strands at her nape and lifted them on top of her head. He arranged her hair into a loose bun, his lips so close to her own that she wanted to rise up on her toes and place a kiss on them.

Especially when he paused and closed his eyes.

"What is it?"

"You smell so good."

The longing in his voice unraveled her resistance.

He dropped his hands, letting her hair fall back over her shoulders, and opened his eyes. She was caught in his gaze.

Slowly, he lowered his head to hers, taking her lips in a gentle kiss.

It was sweet, tender and testing. And short. He drew back and looked at her, then kissed her again, his lips opened, lingering.

He tasted of mint and citrus. She threaded her fingers through his hair, angled her mouth and deepened the kiss.

A low moan escaped his throat as his arms came around her and his hands slid down her spine. The feel of his muscled arms, of his hard length pressed against her stomach, turned her desire up to molten lava. But it was more than physical need. It felt…like an ache in her heart.

Still kissing him madly, she walked backward toward the dressing room and he followed, his hands cupping her bottom.

"You want the costume, then?" the clerk asked.

Cold air hit Piper's body as Neil jerked away from her and spun to face the woman.

The clerk was eyeing them with distaste, arms folded across her chest. "You need to pay for it before you—" She raised her brows and glared pointedly between them and the dressing room.

Piper's blood turned to ice. The woman made it clear she thought Piper was playing the role of naughty chambermaid for her lover.

Neil cleared his throat and reached into his back pocket to pull out a wallet. “Sure. We’ll ta—”

Piper assumed her haughtiest expression. “I’ll need work shoes, too. Black. Size seven.” She returned the clerk’s disapproving glare and raised one brow for good measure. If the woman hadn’t scurried off, Piper would’ve shooed her away with a wave of her fingers.

Neil swung around again to face her. “Remind me not to get on your bad side.” One corner of his mouth quirked up.

He wasn’t disapproving, but still Piper narrowed her eyes at him. “You’re assuming I have a good one. See if they have black stockings, tall.” She flung the dressing-room curtain aside and sauntered in before Neil noticed her face was hot and her breathing was uneven.

“One pair of black stockings coming up.” He gave her legs a smoldering look, then saluted her and disappeared into the back of the store.

She pressed her palms to her cheeks.

If that woman hadn’t interrupted them, Piper’s thong would be down around her ankles and Neil would probably be thrusting inside her, taking her against the wall… She closed her eyes and sat on the chair. The past four months she’d had no trouble remaining celibate. Now she’d almost done it with Neil in a public dressing room? What had happened to her vow to be good?

Good was a relative thing, it seemed, when it came to Neil Barrow.

ONCE THEY REACHED her new hotel, Neil instructed the cab driver to pull into the parking garage and drive all the way to the back. Past a row of large metal dumpsters was a door with a sign that read Hotel Employees Only.

As she exited the cab, Piper grabbed the bag of cooled Cuban food. Hopefully the room had a microwave. If she couldn't have Neil—and she shouldn't—she intended to eat every bite of the *ropa vieja.*

But Neil got out, as well. At her questioning look, he gestured for her to precede him. "I'll see you to the elevator."

A security guard waiting by the employees' door let them in and greeted Neil. Did he know everyone in Miami? The guard's leather gun holster squeaked as he led them down a narrow corridor to a lift twice the size of a regular hotel elevator. When they stepped on, the guard remained behind, but shook Neil's hand with a silent nod. The doors swished closed and they were alone. She could feel his gaze on her, but she couldn't look at him right now. Her emotions were all tangled and confused.

Undeterred, he brushed the hair off her shoulder and touched his lips to the sensitive spot on her neck. "Piper."

She shivered and closed her eyes as he softly nibbled his way to her lobe.

"I want you," he said.

The lift stilled and the doors opened. With a low moan, Neil straightened and ushered her into a corridor that led them past the busy, crowded kitchens to another larger lift.

He pointed at the wide metal door. "These are the service elevators that lead to the guest-room floors.

You have the room number, right?" She nodded and he pressed the up button. They waited in silence. Then he sighed and turned to face her. "I don't want to go back to my hotel tonight."

She understood. Decision time. She'd fought hard to change her ways the past four months. But, oh, how she wanted to give in to the fever she had for this man.

It was just one night, right? The tabloids already thought they were lovers, so it wasn't her rep she had to worry about. So why did she hesitate? She searched his eyes. Gentle brown eyes filled with desire, filled with want.

He framed her face, his lips almost meeting hers. A nearby door swung open and Neil jerked aside to face the lift as a woman pushing a laundry cart bustled past them.

Piper smiled, feeling like the schoolgirl she'd never had a chance to be, let alone hiding a secret boyfriend. Maids weren't supposed to fraternize with guests; Neil was still protecting her. But then, as they both stood there, facing the lift, his hand found hers and captured her fingers in rough warmth. A simple gesture. One of friendship and solidarity. Telling her without words that he would be okay with whatever she decided.

The lift dinged and the doors opened. She stepped inside and he let go of her hand.

She stood opposite him and the elevator doors started to close.

Celibacy was overrated. She grabbed his shirt and yanked him inside the open car.

He used the momentum to plaster her against the

wall and take her mouth. Deep. Hungry. She caressed the muscles rippling beneath his T-shirt, his shoulder blades moving as he held her in his arms. The elevator slowed to a stop, opened and they stumbled forward, barely pausing to find the right room. Neil bumped against the door to the suite as she ran her hands over his hot flesh.

The door swung back. Neil broke away from her, his chest heaving.

Ragi stood in the doorway. She glanced from Piper to Neil and back again. "I'm sorry to interrupt. But you said to meet you with the key."

Right. She'd forgotten. Grimacing, she looked up at Neil. Maybe this was for the best. She wasn't exactly known for making smart decisions.

Neil shrugged, giving her a rueful grin. "Good night, Piper." He nodded to Ragi. "Ms. Bhagat." He headed for the lift.

The farther away he got, the heavier her heart felt. She was supposed to return to London tomorrow. She'd never see him again. She couldn't bear that.

"Wait!"

Neil stopped and turned, brows raised.

Piper ran up to him. "You said you would take me to the Florida Keys…"

His lips curved up in a slow smile.

7

IF NEIL HAD ever fantasized about being alone on a boat with a drop-dead sexy lingerie model, he'd probably have pictured her tall, tanned body in a bikini, sunbathing out on the bow. She'd be leaning back on her elbows, hair blowing in the wind while she gave him a sultry smile. Maybe she'd bring him a beer and caress his manly biceps while he kept watch over the helm.

A guy could dream.

What he got instead was a woman he'd snuck out of a hotel, who was wearing a thrift-shop maid's uniform under a bulky orange life vest, clinging white-knuckled to the rail and looking so green she could pass for the Wicked Witch of the West. And yet, even then, she was remarkably beautiful.

"You okay?" Neil frowned at Piper as mist from a wave sprayed over the starboard side.

"Fine." She smiled, but it looked more like a grimace.

The main sail and jib were slacking a bit. He checked

wind speed and direction and turned the wheel, tacking into the breeze.

The weather was perfect—he'd monitored the forecast and filed a float plan with the coast guard before picking Piper up this morning. Blue skies, a few puffy clouds and a warm sun overhead. Traveling at about six and a half to seven knots, they'd made good time and were already in the Intracoastal Waterway. The wind was minimal; the water was relatively calm.

But a good sailor, Piper was not.

He handed her a bottle of water from the cooler. "You've been on a boat before, right?"

"Of course." She waved at the ocean. "Dozens of times."

He gave her his skeptical look.

She rolled her eyes. "Okay, maybe only a couple of times. Once on a yacht the size of my London flat. And we tooled around an empty bay while I downed lots of yummy champagne. Is that what you wanted to know?"

He grinned. Even weak and nauseated she was a wiseass.

"Then there was the cruise ship earlier this year," she said quietly.

"You went on a cruise?"

"Working trip, actually."

"Well, being on a large ship is different. I'm sorry about this. If you'd said something we could've driven down."

She shrugged. "I never say no to adventure."

After she'd mentioned the Keys last night, his mind had gone all fuzzy and his breath had caught, thinking of the two of them alone for a couple of days. And a couple of nights.

A secluded bungalow by the beach, soft waves crashing, a ceiling fan circling lazily overhead. Their bodies entwined on cool cotton sheets…

Piper sprang up and bent over the side of their boat, nauseous. Cursing, Neil scanned the waterway to make sure their route was clear, turned the knob to lock the wheel and reached her in time to slip one arm around her waist and hold her hair away from her face. As she straightened, she fell against him, limp.

He carried her to the cushioned bench seat and dropped to one knee at her feet. "Feel better?" He tried to give her a reassuring smile.

She wiped her mouth with the back of her hand. "I'm so sorry you had to see that."

"*You're* sorry? I'm the moron. I should've ditched this idea the minute I saw your face this morning when we arrived at the dock. Hold on a sec." He jogged down to the galley, grabbed a towel and brought it back to her, and then gently brushed her hair behind her ears.

Their gazes met and she covered his hand where he was stroking her cheek. "No. It's not your fault."

He stared up at her, amazed. Instead of whining and complaining—which she had every right to do—she was trying to reassure him. The guys in his platoon would call her a salty dog.

While she rinsed her mouth with the water, he shook his head, wanting to kick himself for doing this to her. "We could turn back, or heave to, but I don't think that would help the situation." This morning, the Miami skyline had risen above the horizon like tall and short blocks on a graph. Deep shady purple on the west half of the buildings contrasted with blinding sunlight reflected on the east. Ahead of them now, he could barely see a dark green strip of land to the northeast. "We're almost halfway there. But I've got some seasick meds in the first-aid kit. Why don't you go below deck and lie down?"

"No. That would make things worse. I'll be all right."

"Are you sure? It's going to be almost dark before we get to Key Largo."

"Key Largo?"

"Yeah, like the song?"

She frowned. "The song?"

"You know...Bogie and Bacall?"

She still looked confused.

Great. Now he felt super old. "Never mind." But more words of the old hit song came back to him. Something about a sweet surrender and giving the guy her heart. She hadn't even been born when that song came out. Although, thinking about it, he wasn't even sure *he'd* been born.

She propped her arms on the edge of the stern, looking out over the water. "It's beautiful here. Might we see a dolphin, do you think?"

"It's very likely," he replied. "Dolphins, gulls, pelicans. The real treat is the reefs. The coral is amazing." He considered her for a moment. "Do you snorkel?"

She wrinkled her nose. "No."

"No problem. We only have a couple of days. Maybe next time." Then he caught what he'd said. Next time?

As if they would come back together at some point? As if they had a future. It was crazy.

But the words had just shot out of his mouth without his brain engaging first.

She had transferred her gaze back to him, though her expression revealed nothing.

"I meant, maybe *you* could come back sometime. You know, when you're in the area again."

"I'd like that."

Those luminous light green eyes of hers… He should walk away, instead he moved closer to her. The life vest was awkward between them. He raised his hand to caress her cheek and she pressed into his palm.

The bow of the boat tossed up, spraying saltwater over them, and Piper jerked back, fear written on her face.

He jumped to his feet, unlocked the wheel and tacked starboard. Another boat had come within a couple dozen yards of hitting them. What had he been thinking to leave the helm for so long? The woman turned his brain to mush.

The sooner he got her off this boat, the better.

PIPER AWOKE SLOWLY to a man who was calling her name, his strong arms lifting her. When she opened her eyes, she saw feathery palm fronds silhouetted against a lavender sky. The sun was a bright orange ball turning the horizon pinkish red as it sank into the water.

"Beautiful," she murmured, and laid her head on Neil's shoulder. The faint whiff of his musky cologne made her nuzzle her face against his jaw.

“Let’s get you on solid ground, okay?” He unhooked her life vest and tugged it off, then practically carried her off the boat and onto a dirt path. Her hand rested on his chest. His T-shirt was damp, clinging to the hard muscle beneath. She could feel the outline of his dog tags.

“How are you feeling?” His voice was soft, so full of concern.

She assessed herself. Her headache was gone and she felt…ravenous. She happily smiled at him. “Much improved.”

His expression showed his relief. “Good. Our bungalow is this way.”

“Bungalow?”

He kept his arm around her waist as they made their way down the dirt path to an older lady with deeply weathered skin, in white capris and a bright yellow T-shirt that read Largo Cottages. She handed Neil a key attached to a large plastic key chain. “I saw your boat sailing up. I’m Jen. Welcome to Key Largo.” She gestured to the pathway that led toward a thick copse of trees. Piper could see a couple of lights twinkling through the darkness.

“Oh, Neil. How did you find this place?”

Neil shrugged and gave a teasing grin. “I know a guy.” He took the key from the lady. “Thanks, Jen.” Then he touched Piper’s arm. “I’ll get the bags.” He jogged back to the boat, climbed in and returned with her case and his duffel. He took Piper’s hand and steered her toward the woods.

Piper scanned her pretty surroundings. The boat

was moored at a short wooden dock alongside a thin piece of land that jutted out into the blue bay, shored up with white boulders. Large palm trees with wide green fronds lined the path, and colored lanterns were strung from tree to tree, leading them to a white wooden cabin nestled in dense tropical foliage.

From the exterior, the cabin seemed small, but inside, the main room was spacious. Cool green walls and bamboo furniture covered with thick white cushions surrounded a glass fireplace, and there was an efficiency kitchen outfitted with modern appliances.

Neil followed her down the hall and set their bags just inside the bedroom door. A four-poster bed covered with sumptuous white linens dominated the room. Opposite the loo was a set of French doors that led out to the beach.

As she ran her palm over the thick comforter, he stuck his hands into the pockets of his cargo shorts and leaned against the door frame. "Hungry?"

She smiled. "Starving."

"Good. You want to freshen up while I get some dinner?"

She peeked into the airy bathroom. There was a large jet tub as well as a shower. "A hot bath does sound lovely. But where do you propose to get food?"

"There's a restaurant and a store not far down the road. Any requests?"

"Anything you bring is fine."

He nodded and turned to go.

"Neil."

He halted and glanced back.

"Thank you."

His eyes darkened. "I'll be back in an hour."

After a hot soak in the tub, Piper threw on a sundress and then explored the grounds around the cottage. Off the kitchen was a small deck with a round table and two chairs, and steps leading to the beach.

It was getting dark already, but the same kind of lanterns that had brightened the pathway from the dock were strategically placed around the white sandy beach. Surrounding this spot was a forest of mangrove trees.

There were a couple of Adirondack chairs beneath an umbrella close to the softly lapping water, and a waning moon was bright enough to see the hammock slung between two larger palm trees. Compared to, say, her ex Francois's cliff-side villa in Monaco, this little getaway might best be described as quaint. But it was quiet. Secluded. Perfect.

Neil had brought her to a private paradise.

Walking back to the deck, she heard the key in the lock, and the door to the bungalow opened and then closed again. She padded in just as Neil was setting several full plastic bags on the kitchen counter. He turned and their gazes met.

Amazed that she was so lucky to be here with Neil, she simply studied the man. He wasn't classically handsome. Just an average-looking bloke, really. Of course, the arms were nicely muscular, the chest impressive. But none of that was what really drew her to him. It was something in him. Something she'd felt from that first dinner with him. Something that made her want to be wrapped in his arms and stay there forever.

Oh, please. She sounded like a sentimental twit.

His gaze never wavered as she closed the distance between them, stopping a mere inch from him. "I find that I'm suddenly not so hungry," she said with a kiss.

Needing no further encouragement, he cradled the back of her head in his palm and slanted his mouth over hers, enveloping her in a sensual kiss. Her arms went round his neck, and she rose on tiptoe to fit her body to his. His kisses grew more passionate, more desperate as he lifted her and headed for the bedroom.

Melting into his embrace, she circled her legs about his waist, hooked her ankles at the small of his back and buried her fingers in his short hair. She wanted him—needed him. Had since she'd met him, she realized now.

He bumped against the end of the bed and bent to lower her onto the soft comforter. Without removing his lips from hers he reached under her dress and slipped her knickers down. But then he gave a frustrated grunt when he had to struggle to untangle her legs from around his waist to get them off her.

Mmm, the look on his face as he accomplished his mission—raw hunger. Piper felt exposed, lying there propped on her elbows, waiting for him. But she also felt exhilarated. Anticipating. Needing.

He glanced up to meet her eyes, then fell to his haunches, placed his hands on the insides of her thighs, and slowly lapped his tongue against her.

Her head fell back as a keening moan escaped her throat. For the next while she knew nothing, saw nothing. She could only think, *Neil. Neil. Neil.* And *Yes.*

And *Do that again*. And *More*. He was an expert. A master. A god.

Pleasure built, winding tighter and tighter inside her. She was making silly embarrassing sounds, lifting her hips, giving herself to him, until she felt consciousness leave her. She was everywhere and nowhere. She was in the room, but not.

Slowly, she could hear herself breathing. Heard the sounds outside. Cicadas chirping, ocean waves roaring. She opened her eyes. The ceiling fan whirled overhead.

"I wish you could see how amazing you look right now." Neil sat back on his heels, kneeling before her.

But it was she who should be worshipping him. He was still dressed. That just wasn't right.

She sat up and reached for the hem of his T-shirt, yanking it over his head. Being a smart man, he understood her urgency and lifted his arms, then began shedding his shorts and boxers. She got a good look at his impressive erection while he rolled on a condom.

She shuffled backward as he rose over her, stalking her like a large cat, his dog tags swinging. She watched the flexing of his taut muscles, arms, abs, thighs. His tanned skin gave evidence of his dangerous occupation. A four-inch scar across his abdomen. A round puckered one on his left shoulder. A tat on his right upper arm. It was the SEAL trident with a date below it. She ran her fingers over the tattoo, then to the smattering of dark hair on his chest that arrowed down to his straining erection.

His lips curved in a feral smile as he hovered over her on hands and knees. "Take off your dress."

With a smile she grabbed the edge of the sundress and tugged it up and over her head. She pulled it free from her hair and tossed it…somewhere. Then she bent her arms behind her to unclasp her bra.

"No." His eyes blazed, riveted on her.

"No?"

He finally lifted his gaze from her breasts and looked into her eyes. "I want to enjoy this a bit." He ran the back of his hand over the lacy edge of her bra. "This is one of those Desiree's Desire lingerie things, right?"

"Of course." Her nipples were hard peaks, and she drew in a breath slowly, anticipating his touch.

He lowered his head and placed his mouth on her belly button, kissing his way to her ribs. He stopped when he reached the edge of her bra and groaned. "Never thought I'd say this, but I think purple is my new favorite color."

"You mean Pleasurable Plum?"

He grinned. "Yeah." He took her nipple in his mouth through the bra, gently suckling, and then switched to the other breast.

She placed her palms to his head, kissed his temples.

He sank onto her then, one knee between her legs, while he tugged her bra straps down. She reached behind her and unhooked the clasp, flinging the bra away.

"Oh, Piper." With a worshipful expression, he cupped her breasts, drawing a nipple deep into his mouth.

Now. She needed to feel him inside her now. She tightened her legs around his waist and he braced himself on one forearm and held her gaze as he slowly filled her.

He groaned and closed his eyes, then kissed her. As he moved over her, his thrusts became more and more urgent. The more powerful they became, the greater the pleasure she felt. Her hips rose to meet him, encouraging him. His lips returned to her breasts and she finger combed the soft brown curls at his nape. She felt herself peaking and cried out, lost in all the sensation as her world rocked.

His arms held her close and he thrust one last time, then stiffened, burying his face between her breasts.

Gulping a deep breath, he let it out on a groaning exhalation and rolled to her side, pulling her against him. He lay panting, and ran a hand through his hair.

For a few moments she watched his chest rise and fall, listened to his heart pounding beneath her ear. Her fingers played with the hair on his chest and traced the path leading lower to his groin. She teased the indentation between hip and thigh. "Let's do that again."

He barked a laugh. "Give me a few minutes. I'm old."

She shrugged. "Not so old."

He slanted her a disbelieving look, then patted her butt. "Be right back." He slid out from beneath her and padded into the loo.

She hugged the pillows while he washed up, feeling more relaxed and content than she had in a long while.

When he came back to bed she snuggled against him once more. Reaching between them, she cupped him, stroking him to hardness. "Mmm, see? Not old."

He moaned and turned to lie half over her. "Two can play at that." Holding her gaze, he found her again and caressed softly with his fingers. Then he kissed her longingly, slowly. "Tell me one thing about yourself nobody else knows," he said as he nibbled her lips.

She blinked. "Why?"

"Why? Because I want to know you."

"Neil." Why should they get to know anything more about each other? This was supposed to be a quick fling. A rebellious getaway for a couple of days of mindless sex until they both had to return to the real world. She wiggled her hips and grinned. "I'd say you know me very well."

"Just one—" he trailed kisses up her jaw "—little—" a lingering kiss on her mouth "—thing."

She growled. "Okay, fine." But what could she tell him? He wanted to know something that no one else knew? That left the field wide-open. Nobody knew anything about her at all except Ragi. And Ragi didn't pry. No one really knew her…

"I…love chocolate."

His brows shot up. "Really?" His tone was sarcastic. "Nobody else in the world knows that?"

She shrugged. "Your turn. Tell me something about you that no one else knows."

He hesitated, frowning.

She encircled his cock. "Tell me."

"Okay, okay." He placed his hand over hers. "It's been… I haven't… It's been a long while since…"

"Since you had sex? Hah!" She laughed. "Been a while, huh? What? A whole three days?"

His smile faded. "What makes you say that?"

She shrugged.

He moved off her and his jaw muscle ticked. "It's been over a year."

Right. Sure. Maybe he'd been stranded on a deserted island. "Whatever. It doesn't matter." She scooted closer to lean over him and placed her hand on his chest, raining kisses everywhere she touched.

"It matters to me. I don't lie."

Raising her head, she met his gaze. "Everybody lies sometimes. But I don't mind. We both know what this is."

He stared at her hard. "You're awful cynical for twenty-three."

"That's not cynicism, that's realism."

"Wow. You've really been burned, huh?"

Burned? She'd been scorched to ashes. But not the way he thought. She sighed. "Well, that's quite a mood killer." She swung her legs to the side of the bed, grabbing up her dress. She had not come to the Keys to be psychoanalyzed.

Sitting up, he rearranged the sheet to cover himself from the waist down. His expression grew serious as he continued to stare at her. "What's going on here? You're angry with me?"

"Why should I be angry?" Wait. Was she angry? What did any of it matter?

He heaved a sigh and got up to find his boxers.

She slipped her dress back on, folded her arms over her chest and paced away.

As he stepped into his underwear, she pushed open the French doors and wandered down to the soft warm sand. The half-moon sparkled on the dark water, the waves rolled into the shore.

What had happened to having a simple mindless

fling? How had things suddenly gotten so complicated? All she'd wanted was to take the orgasm train to oblivion, but he'd had to ruin it by pretending she was somebody special to him.

He couldn't have it both ways. He'd either come down to Miami to have some fun, seen her and decided she was a sure thing, or he— He what? Tears stung her eyes. Or he actually cared for her? It hurt how much she wanted that to be true.

But knowing it could never be true hurt even more.

8

WHAT HAD JUST HAPPENED?

Neil continued to stare after Piper's retreating figure. He slipped on his shorts and followed her out to the beach. Somehow he'd even managed to mess this up. Whatever *this* was.

Piper was sitting on the edge of a wide hammock, rocking with her heels in the sand and her arms wrapped around her. More than ever, he got a sense of how vulnerable she really was.

He approached Piper cautiously. Too many ops went south from rushing into unknown territory without proper planning. But what would be the best strategy in a situation like this? He wasn't even sure what the situation was. He sank to his haunches and looked up at her.

"Piper, sweetheart, what's the matter?" He reached up to knuckle a tear off her cheek, but she slapped his hand away.

"I'm not your sweetheart." She turned her face.

He was clueless what to do. But he held his position.

"You don't have to pretend you care about me, okay? I'm a sure thing. Isn't that why you asked me out?"

Huh? She thought he was a player, a guy looking to carve a notch on his bedpost? Neil shifted to one knee, sat back and settled in for an explanation. "Look, I didn't know who you were before I asked you out. But I admit, before dinner that first night, my buddy told me and yeah, okay, I thought maybe I'd get lucky. Since then I've come to… I care about you."

She lifted her chin and glared at him. "You don't even know me." Her tone held a bitter edge.

"I've been trying to get to know you. That's why I asked you to tell me something about yourself."

Still hugging herself, she hunched her shoulders and studied her feet, digging her toes into the sand. "But why would you bother to pretend?"

"Piper, I—" He stared out to sea and let out a frustrated breath. "It's not an act, Piper. I'm attracted to you. And I genuinely like you."

Silence.

Finally, she sniffed and looked at him. "Really?" She didn't sound mad anymore, but he was pretty sure he preferred anger to the disbelief he heard in her tone.

"Yes, please believe me." He wrapped his arms around her and stroked the length of her soft black hair. "Why is that so hard to believe? I don't know many twenty-three year olds who could handle the life you lead. You're obviously a hard worker, long hours, I bet. And you're intelligent."

She huffed, and glanced at him for a second. "How am I intelligent?"

He couldn't help but stare at her luminescent green eyes, her full red lips. "You're smart enough to successfully run your very own lucrative corporation." When she made a face he refused to give up and kept going. "Agent, PR assistant. They're all employees of Piper, Inc., right? That's a business."

She cocked her head, her brows drawing together. "I never thought of it like that. I always figured *they* were running *me*."

"Well." He swallowed. "That's not really true."

"Hmm." She met his gaze. "Maybe you're right." She shifted closer till their mouths were almost touching. He was totally confused. He would never understand women. One minute she was furious, the next she acted as though she was going to—

She kissed him. Before he could react, she launched herself off the hammock, pushing him to his back on the soft sand. Her tongue swept into his mouth and his erection went from half-mast to mission ready.

Straddling his thighs, she unzipped his shorts, peeled down his underwear and enveloped him in her warm wet mouth.

Words of thanksgiving he usually reserved for the safe completion of a mission filled his mind as his whole body stiffened.

But he knew something still wasn't right with her.

"Piper, wait." In one motion he sat up, gripped her upper arms and lifted her off him.

"What?" She scowled at him.

"I just—" Why couldn't he seem to get anything right with this woman?

"Isn't this what we came here for?" she asked.

"What?" He yanked his shorts back up. "No. I—I mean yes, but…only if you want to." He rubbed the back of his neck. "With *me*. Not because you think that's what's expected of you."

"Oh." She blinked and seemed to be thinking that through. A trembling smile curved her lips. "So it'd be okay with you if we just lie here and look at the stars?"

"Okay."

"Okay." She grinned and lay down on her back. With one hand she made trails in the sand with her fingers, her other arm tucked behind her head.

Cursing to himself for absolutely never understanding women, he did the same, putting one arm behind his head as a pillow. What was the matter with him? Neil stared at the stars and the swaying palm trees. He must be a secret masochist. This was not how he'd seen this night turning out.

"The air is so warm here." Her voice was soft, reflective.

"It's no French Riviera, but it'll do."

"You've been to the French Riviera?"

He chuckled. "Not exactly a hot spot for terrorism. But I figured you had."

"Yes. But this is just as nice."

"Yeah." He wouldn't dare disagree. "I'll probably retire here someday. Buy a little fishing boat. Dive the reefs."

Her stomach growled.

"You hungry?"

"Yes."

He jumped up and extended his hand to help her to her feet. Within minutes he'd heated the thick sandwiches he'd ordered from the barbecue place down the road. Content, they sat on the deck while they ate and talked about all the places she'd modeled.

"The Desiree's Desire catalogue shoots are at the studio in New York, but for our calendars we've shot in some quite exotic locales. Bora Bora, Fiji, the Maldives…"

"Man, what I wouldn't give to dive at any of those places."

She shrugged. "I never got to see much more than the beach and the inside of my hotel room."

"That's crazy. Why not?"

"I didn't have time. But I wouldn't have gone in the water in any case."

"You don't like the water?"

"I'm not a good swimmer." She picked up her sandwich. "You should go to Fiji, though."

He lifted a shoulder. "Maybe someday. I mostly go where I'm told nowadays."

"And where is that?"

"Oh, you know. The usual hotbeds of insurrection and chaos. A lot of sand, not so many beaches." He smirked.

She frowned. "You serve your country with honor. You constantly risk your life. Yet you can joke about it."

"I chose this life. Got no reason to complain."

She popped the last bite in her mouth and licked her lips. "Mmm. That was so good."

He was keenly aware that she was naked under that

dress. When he brought his gaze back to her eyes, she had one brow raised and was playing with the fork between her teeth. A jolt went from his gut to his cock.

Her chair scraped as she stood and came around the table to stand before him. "I want to have sex with *you*, Neil Barrow."

He held her gaze as she slowly lifted her dress over her head, pulled it past her long hair and dropped it onto the deck.

Neil swallowed past the lump in his throat. Her words were like a balm to his soul. His own wife hadn't wanted him. Had never looked at him the way that Piper was looking at him right now. He didn't know how he'd gotten so lucky to be thrown into the path of this gorgeous woman, but he needed this, needed *her*.

Adrenaline kicked in as if he was heading out for an op. Danger and excitement made his fingers tremble in anticipation. He stood and held her in his arms, walking her backward and then lifting her as he negotiated the steps toward the hammock. He set her down on the edge and kissed her beautiful lips, down her jaw to her neck. Her skin was like silk, and he was conscious of his callused hands as he caressed her arm, circled her waist.

He barely managed to grab a packet from his pocket before she fumbled with his button and zipper and tugged his shorts and briefs down. He'd wanted to go slow, pleasure her first, make it all last. But she hooked her ankles at the small of his back and murmured for him to hurry, that she needed him now.

His fingers shook as he rolled on protection. He wanted to say something. Tell her this felt like more than just sex. "Piper." He framed her face and looked deeply into her eyes for a moment. What did he see in their depths? Fear? Pleading? She didn't want this to mean anything more? Still not sure what to say exactly, he opened his mouth, but she captured it with hers and tightened her legs around his back.

As her heat surrounded him, he let it all go. All the worry, the complicated feelings, everything but how good it felt to be inside her.

Right where he wanted to be. He had a strange feeling he would never want to be anywhere else.

9

Piper cried out when he entered her. She combed her fingers through the hair at his nape and held him to her. Her breasts were pressed up against his chest and she felt closer to this strong, gentle man than she'd ever felt to anyone.

Neil had said he cared for her. No one had ever told her that before. Oh, how she wanted to believe him. She kissed his temple, his ear, nibbled at his lobe.

He groaned into her neck, murmured her name over and over again. She was humbled yet proud at the same time that such a good man, an honorable man, wanted to be with her. He rocked his hips and began a steady rhythm. The hammock shook and Piper clung to him, pleasure building anew, but different. This time felt more intimate. She could be herself with him.

That meant a lot to her. It was already more than what any other man she'd been with had given to her. But could she really trust Neil? She wanted to.

One of his hands stroked her cheek, her lips and her

jaw before tangling gently in her hair. She arched her back to encourage him and he quickly pressed kisses to her neck. "Come with me."

His sweetly whispered words undid her. One more stroke, and another, and she came apart, clinging to him. As if her reaction gave him permission to follow, he stiffened in her arms and his head tilted back. His jaw clenched and a groan thundered from his chest. Drawing a shivering breath, he squeezed her to him.

Piper realized she wanted to stay this way forever. With him deep inside her she felt whole, part of something bigger. She rubbed his back and felt goose bumps on his flesh as he shuddered and sighed.

He lifted his head and gazed into her eyes. "Do you know how beautiful you are to me right now?"

She gave a choking laugh. "Yeah, right."

Piper couldn't tell if Neil was only shocked or actually angry at her response. He had that grim, eyes narrowed, jaw-locked look she imagined he got during a dangerous mission.

"Why do you doubt me?"

She scoffed. "Well, look at me! Beautiful? Now?" Her eyes must be puffy and smudged with mascara, her nose was surely red and running and her hair was a tangled mess.

But Neil had said he didn't lie.

"I wish you could see what I see. There's a fire in your eyes that's incredible. And your face…your face is so truthful. Every emotion, every feeling, it's there." He smiled wryly. "I'm glad I've made you so happy."

She swatted at him, but he quickly avoided her move.

"You are beautiful, Piper, but not just because of your looks. You're beautiful because you gave me everything, including your trust."

Piper's breath caught. Ever since Ms. H had discovered her and brought her to London, Piper had been told she was beautiful. But being valued for something she'd had no part in creating meant nothing.

Something took root in her chest at Neil's words. A tiny spark. She buried her face in his neck so he wouldn't see the truth of it in her eyes.

NEIL WOKE WITH a start.

It was still dark. Waves crashed and a soft breeze blew in from the beach. There were the usual tankers and lit oil rigs out in the Gulf, but no bright lights flashed. No boat horns sounded, no animals called or birds screeched. He lay still, thinking maybe he'd dreamed about a mission. Then the mattress shook.

Piper.

Rubbing a hand over his eyes, he rolled to face her, but she had her back to him. She was curled into a tight ball, sleeping on the edge of her side of the bed. He scooted close against her spine, gently moving thick strands of hair off her wet face.

Crying in her sleep?

During an op, a guy caught sleep whenever he could. Even standing up, if he had to. And he always knew his platoon had his back. He'd seen a couple of guys jerk awake with a nightmare or two. Maybe even yell out. Hell, he probably had himself. But to actually cry while sleeping? What monsters haunted her dreams?

He lightly touched her shoulder. "Piper?"

As he stroked her arm, her body lost its tension, and eventually she uncurled a bit. When he heard her sigh softly, he slid his arm around her waist and snuggled in beside her.

The next time Neil opened his eyes, the sun shone dimly. But he was alone in bed. Looking through the open French doors, he found Piper standing at the edge of the surf. The Gulf sparkled like a sapphire beyond her, and the sun at her back illuminated her caramel-colored skin and black hair. She wore short white shorts and a lime-green tank top. After a moment she turned and shaded her eyes with her hand to watch a flock of pelicans soaring just above the ocean's surface.

Throwing back the sheet, he climbed out of bed, his knees and ankles protesting as usual. He debated putting on some coffee, but the desire to be with Piper won out. So he slipped on his swim trunks and tromped out to the beach, encircling her in his arms from behind. "Good morning."

She gripped his forearms and leaned her head into the crook of his neck. "It is. It's beautiful here. Thank you for bringing me."

Renewed guilt settled in for subjecting her to the boat ride. "I was thinking we'd rent a car and drive back to Miami. It'd only take a couple of hours, so we'd have more time here tomorrow before we have to head out."

"But what about your boat?"

He shrugged. "I'll have someone return it to Miami."

She turned in his arms. "That's very sweet. Thank you."

Yep. That was him. Sweet. Nice. So much for no more Mr. Nice Guy. But who had he been kidding? He couldn't be someone he wasn't. He smiled. "Let's eat. I make a mean egg-white omelet."

She returned his smile. "Sounds delicious."

As they headed into the bungalow, he took her hand. Her soft, slim fingers wrapped around his and he squeezed. Something about the action felt as though they'd been walking side by side like this for years.

As he started cooking, she peeked over his shoulder until he finally asked if she would prefer to take over. She confessed that she didn't know how to do more than push a button on a microwave. So he taught her. Chopping a few veggies, cracking a couple of eggs, grating cheese. What pan to use. She was a quick and eager student, and Neil felt…relevant.

Not that what he did as a SEAL wasn't vital. He knew his actions affected lives, specifically the lives of his team during an op. He knew he was needed. But it wasn't the same as making a difference to one specific person. Especially one who looked at him as if he'd just rocked her world by showing her how to chop an onion.

When they sat down at the little table, she dug in and devoured every bite. Maybe her restless sleep last night had just been a matter of eating too late. He hoped so. But it wasn't likely. Not with the tears he'd seen.

Neil decided against bringing up her nightmare. After cleaning the kitchen together, they parted; he headed outside and stretched out on the hammock. Piper walked down the hall to the bedroom.

He stuck his hands behind his head and closed his

eyes. But after a quarter-hour or so, she didn't join him. He kept a one-eyed surveillance on the bungalow. Maybe she'd gone back to bed? Or she was making phone calls?

He quite interrogating himself and tried to relax, irritated with himself for speculating. If she needed time alone, he'd give her space.

Then she appeared at the French doors and his heart actually skipped a half beat.

She pointed her phone at him. "Say cheese." With a mischievous grin, she snapped his picture, and then headed for one of the Adirondack chairs.

He extended a hand. "Swing with me?"

She didn't hesitate. She veered toward him and climbed in beside him. He made room for her, sliding an arm beneath her. She turned and snuggled against him, but kept one long leg hanging off the side to rock them. She held up the phone again and took a photo of the two of them.

"Okay, no more." He gently nudged her phone away.

With a sigh, she tossed it into the soft sand and then fingered the tattoo on his arm. "That's the trident you were telling me about that first night, right?"

"Yes."

"And the date? 9-13-1972."

"The day my uncle was killed."

She nodded, and they were silent for a while. He was glad she didn't try to sympathize or analyze, or even make him talk about it. It was what it was.

"No tattoos on you, I noticed. Because of your career?" he asked.

"Too right. I'm contractually obligated not to get one."

"Besides liking chocolate, tell me something else about you that no one knows."

At first he thought she wouldn't answer. He'd interrogated enemy informants that had given up hideout locations easier than this.

"My real name is Anju," she said quietly.

He blinked and turned his head to look into her exotic eyes. "Anju. That's a beautiful name."

Her gaze drifted away to the waves in the Gulf. "Mrs. H said I had to change it."

"Who's Mrs. H?"

Her face scrunched up and she squirmed until she'd settled on her side, pillowing her head on his arm. "I'm really knackered."

He noted she hadn't answered his question. But he wasn't going to push it. "*Knackered?* Is that a word?" He grinned and winked, and it worked. She smiled and playfully slapped his chest.

"You Yanks would say tired."

"How about a nap, then?" He traced a path along her arm and placed a kiss on her forehead.

But they didn't sleep.

As the tide slowly came in, they watched a flock of white ibis wander in from the copse of mangrove trees and wade into the surf. Their long, curved orange bills poked around in the wet sand catching insects and crayfish.

The water was calling to him, so Neil got up and waded past the waves before diving in, swimming out far enough to catch glimpses of a pod of dolphins. He called to her to join him, but she wouldn't wade any farther than knee deep. So he swam back and splashed her and they played in the surf.

The sounds of her shrieks and laughter melted his heart as she ran from him.

He caught up to her and scooped her into his arms, pretending to carry her out to sea. She screamed and pounded his chest, but she was laughing, head back, long hair lifting in the wind.

Their mouths met in a soft, sweet kiss, and she cupped his cheek and opened to him. Their tongues teased and lapped until he stumbled and landed on his knees in the sand. With a shout she tumbled out of his arms and rolled to her stomach. She stayed that way, sifting her fingers through the tiny grains.

With her legs kicking up and down on the sand, she looked so pleased and carefree. Then he pictured her on the hammock last night, those same legs wrapped around his hips as she came apart in his arms.

Without thinking, he began molding the damp sand into a fort.

"What are you doing?"

He gave her a funny look. "Building a sandcastle."

"Oh…you don't need special tools for that?" She watched him, tilting her head.

"You've never built a sandcastle before?"

She froze. "When would I have? Other than flying over the ocean when I left India, I'd never seen a beach until I posed for my first swimsuit shoot."

"How old were you when you started modeling? I

saw you were on the cover of some teen magazine. You looked pretty young."

"I was fifteen when I started modeling for department store websites. Seventeen when I got my first magazine cover."

"Fifteen." He whistled.

She shrugged. "Most of the other girls were younger than me. I had a lot of catching up to do."

He packed sand, shaping it into a tower as best he could, and then building a wall for a sniper to hide behind.

She watched him intently, studying his movements.

"You want to help?" he asked.

She nodded, her eyes twinkling. He jogged over to the bungalow for cups and bowls to use as molds and some utensils for shoveling and shaping. He had to show her how to carve out a moat. "Tell me about growing up in India."

She stilled, her gaze concentrated on packing a bowl with sand. "You've heard of the caste system?"

"Sure, but it's illegal now, right?"

She glared at him. "That doesn't prevent discrimination."

He nodded. "Just like the Civil Rights Act didn't automatically stop racism."

She was quiet for a while, continuing to pack sand and then dumping the bowl. Neil waited.

"I am—was—Dalit. One of the untouchables." She was using a spatula to shape a wall and didn't even look up.

Ah. Maybe this was the stuff of her nightmares. "That must've been difficult for you and your family."

She stopped fiddling with the spatula. "Yes."

"Were you—" He measured his next words carefully. He knew the violence that discrimination could provoke. Knew a guy in his platoon who'd been beaten when he was younger by a bunch of morons out looking for a fight. Maybe he should let it go. Change the subject. "Were you—or someone you love—hurt?"

Her brows crinkled. "Someone I love. Yes."

A rage flamed up like hot embers doused with gas. He wanted to fly to India, track down whoever had hurt her loved one and beat them to a pulp. She'd been just a kid. And he wished he could've been there for her. The words *I'm sorry* seemed disgustingly inadequate. But he said them anyway.

She stood and brushed sand off her legs. "I think you should teach me to swim." She marched toward the water.

Message received. She didn't want to talk about it.

He jumped to his feet and caught up to her. "You sure you want to do this?"

She bit her bottom lip and stared out at the waves. Then she looked at him and stuck out her chin. "Yes." She took a tentative step into the water, then reached back and grabbed his hand. "Don't let go, okay?"

"I won't." He tried squeezing her hand to encourage her as they waded farther ahead. She hesitated every time a wave slammed her, and she almost lost her footing twice. Her hand gripped his so tightly that her nails were digging into his skin.

Once the water was waist high she refused to budge.

"The thing is," Neil coaxed, "if you can get past the break of the waves, they won't knock you around so much."

She stared at him for what seemed like several minutes. "All right. That sounds logical."

Holding on to her wrist, he helped her fight past the break until the water was up to her chest. The calmer water seemed to relax her.

She gave him a trembling smile. "This isn't so bad." Finally taking her gaze off him, she scanned the sparkling ocean and the horizon. "I'm still not sure—" She shrieked suddenly and jerked out of his grasp.

In her face he saw pure panic just before she disappeared under the water. What was happening?

"Piper!" He dived, reaching for her, but she was gone. There was a strong undertow he'd underestimated.

Feeling his anxiety rise, he ignored it and dived in the direction of the undertow, and thankfully felt her legs. A powerful sense of relief, one he'd never felt before, soared through him. Thanking every deity he could name, he grabbed on and dragged her to him, then brought them both to the surface.

She spluttered and thrashed about, fighting him.

"Piper, listen to me. Focus. You're okay. I've got you. It's Neil."

She dragged in a breath and coughed for several seconds. Good. She was okay.

He slipped his arm around her and tucked her head against his shoulder, then led her to shore with every last ounce of strength he had. Within seconds he had her on the sand on her side, in the recovery position.

She was still coughing quite a bit and had vomited seawater. Shaking and dazed, she reared up and clung to him, sobbing.

He held her close, shaking a little himself.

"Something bit me. I tried to hop away. Then the water dragged me and I didn't know which way was up."

"Shh, it's all right. You're fine. Everything's okay." He kept up the soothing words as he lifted her into his arms and carried her into the house. He didn't set her down—couldn't even if he'd wanted to—as he turned on the shower and stepped in with her.

Shedding suits and washing the sand and saltwater off, he slowly lowered her to her feet, and her grip on him eased a fraction. They stayed under the warm water for who knows how long, until, eventually, she let out a long sigh and lifted her head from his chest.

She raised her right foot and pointed to a red mark on the outside edge. "See? I told you something bit me."

Neil knew she was focusing on the mundane to avoid thinking about the monumental. It was a coping technique and a good one. For now. Mortality was a heavy topic. He stepped out of the shower and brought over a towel, swaddled her and carried her from the bathroom to the bed. "Let me see." Kneeling, he took her foot and carefully studied the bite mark. Then he kissed the spot and rubbed his thumb over it. "Probably a crab. I bet he was more scared of you than you were of him."

"I *seriously* doubt that." Sarcasm practically dripped from her words.

He grinned. Her sass was back. He looked into her eyes. "Maybe you're right." He stood and sobered. "This was my fault. I should've—"

"No. Don't even." She reached for his hand, tugged him down beside her. "I'm fully responsible for my own decisions. Don't take away my agency."

"What?"

"It was something my therapist once said. My agency is like my feeling of empowerment. When I blame others, I give them my power. I hadn't really understood it until you tried to take the blame for this just now."

Neil blinked. "You're amazing. You know that, right?"

Her expression softened and her eyes warmed. She pushed at his chest, but then cuddled into him. "Hold me for a while?"

As he did as she'd asked, something took hold inside of him, giving him that power she was talking about. Which was crazy and didn't make any sense because he'd never *not* felt empowered—if he had ever thought about it at all. But Piper seemed to bring out the best in him. And made him believe his life counted for something more than being a SEAL.

WHEN PIPER AWOKE hours later, they ate a late lunch on the deck and fed pieces of orange and mango to a two-foot-long iguana that crashed their impromptu picnic.

"After what happened I thought you might want to leave," Neil ventured.

Piper's mouth dropped open and her eyes widened. "No way."

He grinned, although he still wasn't entirely convinced. "Good. Once we're done with this, I thought we'd get out of here for a bit."

"Where to?"

"You'll see. Get dressed."

He took her to Key Largo's wild bird sanctuary, guessing correctly that she'd enjoy the exotic birds and the idea of a place of refuge for injured or displaced animals. Plus, he wanted to take her mind off what had happened earlier in the ocean.

Piper's eyes sparkled as she wandered around the sanctuary. She found the owner at the visitors' center and asked the woman several insightful questions and the two got into a lengthy conversation.

Neil stood back and watched.

Piper was so much more than he thought most people gave her credit for. Intelligent. Open. Caring.

At one point she glanced over at him and he caught her eye. Her expression relaxed and her gaze warmed. It was a moment of pure connection. As if they were the only two people on the planet.

When they returned to the cottage, she pulled him over to the hammock and slowly tugged off his T-shirt. The sound of the waves and a bird calling did nothing to distract him as she unbuttoned the sheer white blouse she was wearing.

He wanted to tell her to forget about the buttons, but he admitted to himself he was enjoying this—her frankness, her passion, the desire in her eyes. She was the most special, most unique woman he had ever met. He wouldn't have traded this moment for the world.

She bent and eased out of her shorts; the blouse puddled at her feet, her bare breasts full and round, the sight chipping away at his control. Next she peeled off the satin thong and then straddled his lap, rubbing her softness against his hardness.

Neil enfolded her in his arms, wanting to keep her safe within them forever. He could've lost her. No matter what she'd said about agency, it would've been his fault. He squeezed her to him, and then kissed her eyes, her nose, her earlobe. She turned and gave him her mouth, her lips trailing down his jaw, his neck.

She placed her palms on his bare chest and rubbed up and down, then over his shoulders and back. When she reached for the zipper on his shorts, he held her off. "I don't have protection."

With a sly smile, she grabbed her shorts and pulled out a packet. He chuckled.

How much did he love this woman? Then he caught himself. It was just a figure of speech, but…it didn't feel like it.

While he nibbled at her neck, she finished unzipping his shorts. She then ripped the packet open and rolled the condom on, giving his cock a few strokes that made him tighten his grip on her shoulders.

She rose up on the balls of her feet and guided him to her opening. When she sank down onto him, she let out a cry of pleasure. After that, he didn't think about anything else as she moved over him, and together they found their rhythm.

Reverently, he cupped her breasts, and kissed his way

from one breast over her collarbone to her other breast. He gritted his teeth and hung on as she rocked faster, murmuring how much she wanted him. He wanted her just as much, or possibly even more, but he couldn't form the words. He was lost in her, utterly and completely, and it felt good. Very, very good, in fact.

Suddenly, she stopped, stilled in his arms, and a soul-shattering climax roared through them both. Slipping over this edge, this time, with this woman would be something he'd never forget.

When she fell limp against him, he kissed her forehead tenderly and tightened his arms around her.

He wasn't sure how long they sat there, Neil holding her protectively, Piper straddling him, nose buried in his neck, her fingers combing through his hair. He got to his feet and carried her to the hammock and laid her down.

After a quick trip to the bathroom, he joined her. The hammock swung as she curled into his side. As far as he was concerned, they could stay here for the rest of their lives. The world was far away. Her stalker, his own marital mess, none of it mattered for now.

A short while passed before he noticed Piper had gone quiet, her breathing longer and more even. He smiled to himself and stroked her cheek, letting her sleep. He had some thinking to do.

ONCE THEY'D HAD a hot shower, playfully lathering one another, Neil suggested they go out for dinner. Piper agreed, acknowledging she needed to get out into the real world for a few hours.

Neil saving her life had made their private getaway seem even more like a fairy tale. It was too easy to cast Neil as her very own prince, rescuing her from danger. That was fine given their circumstances, but regrettably these circumstances wouldn't last forever. Getting out this afternoon had offered a much-needed dose of reality.

Taking her hand, Neil led her down a well-lit path through the trees to a road with traffic and shops with neon signs. Piper felt as though she'd stepped through a portal. This was the real world, all right.

A few blocks away was a row of restaurants, and Neil headed for a small Italian place. They were seated in a dark, quiet booth in a corner and left alone with menus and a basket of garlic bread.

Piper scooted in close and he tucked her under his arm and caressed her shoulder as they ordered. She slid her hand over his thigh, inching up just enough to torture him. They sipped wine, shared the pasta dish and couldn't keep their hands off each other.

She didn't mean to keep comparing him to other men, but this felt so different from anything she'd experienced.

Francois had been merely expedient. For both of them. Dating Brad had been one publicity-filled outing after another. And it had worked. For him. A few months after he broke it off with her he'd signed on to do a blockbuster film. Hard to imagine she'd thought she loved him for about half a second.

Brad was just a boy compared to Neil. Neil was strength and gentleness. He was patient, but no pushover. He was kind. And…good.

But this feeling she had for him. It couldn't last. Love didn't seem to be an emotion anyone could sustain. Or at least, she couldn't. Was she really saying she was in love with Neil? There was that Prince Charming fantasy kicking in again.

When they got back to the bungalow, they headed straight for the bedroom, leaving a trail of clothes behind them. Neil stood on his side of the bed, yanked the comforter off and threw back the sheet. Naked, she met him in the middle of the mattress, knee to knee, chest to chest. She ran her fingers through his hair and framed his face, opening her mouth over his, kissing his kind lips, pouring everything she couldn't say in words into her kisses. "Make love to me, Neil."

With a groan he laid her down and positioned himself above her. He rolled on protection, nudged her legs apart and thrust. As rushed as they'd been to get back to the bungalow, Neil took his time pleasuring her. He angled his hips as he moved, slowly building the pressure, bringing her to the edge before starting all over again. His weight on his elbows and knees, he placed soft kisses at her temples and jawline as he increased their tempo.

She loved watching his jaw tighten when he came, and his chest expand and fall as he rolled onto his back, breathing hard. And she loved that she could curl up next to him and watch him fall asleep without either of them saying a word. Sometimes no words were needed.

Sometimes, there were words that could never be said.

10

NEIL WOKE IN the middle of the night again. This time Piper's cheek rested on his chest. When she twitched, he brushed her long hair away from her face. Maybe her nightmares were about the water, although that didn't explain the dark dreams last night. So perhaps they were about her loved ones in India. What had happened to them?

He could tell that was the case when she awoke, but she didn't say anything. Did she need to, though?

"You want to talk about it?"

The ocean rumbled. Moonlight spilled in from the French doors. Piper remained silent.

He drew in a deep breath. Felt her cling to him. Maybe he needed to try a different tack. "I sometimes have this nightmare where I'm on the roof of a building, covering the troops on the ground as they enter the city," he said quietly. "And in my nightmare, I can see this ambush about to happen, but I can't pick off the enemy fast enough. And the troops get slaughtered."

"Did that happen?"

"No. Not exactly. But losing even one soldier is unacceptable. I feel as if I should've been able to save them."

She shivered and he gathered her against him again, rubbing her arm. Then more silence.

Well, it'd been worth a try—

"Ms. H would've told you guilt was a waste of time."

"You mentioned Ms. H yesterday."

Neil might not have noticed her subtle hesitation if she hadn't been snuggled against him. "Ms. Hanson. She was my legal guardian until I turned eighteen. And my agent."

Yep. A definite edge to her voice. "Seems as if there might have been a conflict of interest there."

Her shoulder lifted. "She discovered me in India. Brought me to the UK."

He already knew he wasn't going to like Ms. H. He turned to face Piper. "Tell me." He caught the flinch in her eyes.

"There's nothing to tell. I'm grateful to her. She's given me a life I never could've imagined."

There was just a bit too much nonchalance in her tone. Neil raised a brow. "So Ms. H is a saint and everything's peachy. Great." He gave her bottom a playful smack through the sheet. "Guess we can go back to sleep now." He turned his back to her. Punched the pillow. Closed his eyes.

Nothing but quiet stillness behind him. He might've miscalculated that strategy. She didn't owe him anything. But when he started to shift toward her, a soft hand landed on his shoulder, and he pulled her into his arms. "You don't have to talk about it."

She leaned into his chest. "I—" Her voice broke. "I have a brother," she whispered. Her body was stiff, her breath held.

Neil tightened his grip. He'd witnessed interrogations before. Both of prisoners and assets. First order of business: get the names of all the players involved. "What's your brother's name?"

"Nandan."

"Is Nandan older or younger?"

"He was ten the last time I saw him."

The last time she saw him? "Tell me about him."

She brought a hand up to wipe her wet cheeks, and then snuggled into his embrace. "Did I mention to you that I grew up in Delhi?"

"No. But go on."

She cleared her throat. But then she was silent for a long time.

"I've never—" She let out a frustrated growl. "Even Ragi doesn't know this about me."

Neil waited. It had to be her decision.

"Our mother was a…sex worker. It's common for daughters to also…but my mother didn't want that for me. I took care of my brother while she was out, but once he was old enough to go to school, I got to go, too. Then, when I was twelve, my mother—" Piper swallowed. "She got sick. And never got better."

"Your father wasn't around?"

"I never knew my father. But my mother used to tell

me I had his eyes." She turned her face away. "He was a client, I think."

She drew in a deep breath. "After Mata died, Nandan stayed in school and I…begged for a while until I found a job at a food stall in the market. But we were so hungry. All-the-time hungry. And sleeping in the streets. So when Ms. Hanson bought food from me one day and said she wanted to take me to London, I was so happy.

"But she wouldn't let me bring Nandan with us. And he didn't want me to leave him. Ms. H found a family to take him in, and she promised to send money to them every month. I told him I would write to him and he could write to me, but he was inconsolable. He screamed and cried and—" Piper's voice broke again. She was trembling. "He begged me not to leave him."

The obvious pain in her tore at Neil's heart. His chest was wet with her tears.

"I wrote to him every week. And the first year I received three letters from him. All pleading with me to come get him, to let him live with me. But Ms. H said he was better off with a family. We would be gone all the time and he would be alone."

She wiped under her eyes again and sniffed. "The second year the letters stopped. But by then I was traveling to New York a lot and Ms. H said he was fine. I couldn't—couldn't do anything without her permission." Her voice grated with seething anger.

"But when I turned eighteen, she could no longer control me. And I had my own money. I bought a flat and flew to India, planning to bring Nandan back to London to live with me. After three years, I couldn't wait to see him." He heard her sobs, tried holding her closer. "He was gone." She choked on the last word. "The family said he ran away. But—" She pushed away to look at him. "Why didn't they write to tell me? Why didn't they call the police? They did nothing because Ms. H had been sending them money all those years. Oh, Neil." A sob racked her. "I don't know where he is. I've been looking for five years. He thinks I abandoned him."

Neil barely understood the rest of her words but he got the gist of what she was saying. She was afraid her brother was dead or he would've contacted her by now. He caught the words *private investigators* and *reward*, but he let the storm run its course, just holding her until she took a deep breath and let it out on a shivering sigh.

To think Piper had been living with this anguish all these years. The chance that the boy was alive was slim. But Neil couldn't tell her that. He felt touched that she'd confided in him. And he wanted to be there for her, reassure her. More than that. She needed someone in her corner. Her need brought emotions to the surface that he hadn't acknowledged since Lyndsey's betrayal. He needed to be needed.

While Piper slipped into the bathroom to splash water on her face, Neil strategized. She'd had private investigators looking for five years? At best the firm was incompetent, at worst they were just taking her money. There was one other alternative: the boy was dead. And like the family who purportedly took care of him, the investigators didn't want to stop the money flow.

When Piper appeared in the bathroom doorway, he

held out his arms to her and she slipped back into bed beside him. Maybe he'd get the name of the private investigators. And he could ask a buddy of his in the company if there was anything he could do. But no sense in getting her hopes up until he talked to the guy.

PIPER PRESSED HER fingers to her lips and blew Neil a kiss from the hotel's employee entrance. From behind the wheel of the rental, he nodded, the heat in his eyes promising he'd return her kiss in person later that night.

As he drove off, she slipped up to her room in a daze of wonder.

They'd slept late.

After revealing her story to Neil, she'd fallen into an exhausted sleep. It had felt so right to talk to him about her brother. Neil hadn't judged her, or tried to reassure her with lies like the private detectives had.

This morning, too, he didn't seem to want to leave any more than she did. She'd delayed packing, and they'd sat out in the Adirondack chairs on the beach just holding hands and watching the surf until the last possible moment before they had to leave.

By the time he'd secured a rental car it was almost dark.

On the ride home, they drove over a long concrete bridge spanning the distance from Key Largo to the mainland. As they began crossing, Piper became aware that something weird was happening. All the cars ahead of them were pulling over and parking on the shoulder. People exited their cars and stood staring out to sea.

Piper had clutched his arm, worried. "What is it? What's going on?"

Neil grinned and covered her hand. "You're about to witness a spectacular phenomenon." He pulled over between two cars, shut off the engine and opened his door. "Come on." She climbed out and followed him. "There's no more beautiful sunset in the world than the one from the Key Largo Bridge." He placed her in front of him, leaned back against the car and wrapped his arms around her waist.

And he'd been right.

Piper watched with him as the sun painted the sky with the most amazing colors that she'd ever seen. Orange and gold, fuchsia and violet and mauve. Emerald and peach all shining from a giant ball of blazing yellow. Clouds lined in silver touched the horizon and a silhouette of a sailing ship gave the scene a perspective of just how small they all were. How expansive was their universe. A silent awe fell over Piper and the entire group of spectators. It was a moment for reflection, for sharing with someone special. For sharing with Neil. And in the sharing of such a moment, a bond formed that she felt would never be broken.

A profound feeling of reverence overcame her. She was filled with wonder and a sense of timelessness and…true love for the man behind her.

Her lover. Her love.

He'd saved her life.

He'd *changed* her life.

The past two days had been unlike anything she'd ever experienced. The playfulness. The passion. The sense that, for the first time in her life, she had someone who would be there for her. Someone who knew the real her, and…loved her? He hadn't said the words and neither had she. But she was going to tell him tonight.

Just being apart from him for a few hours made her chest ache with longing. To touch him, taste him, even smell him. She could still catch a whiff of his cologne on her now and she inhaled it with a secret smile. She squeezed her eyes closed. *Soon!*

He was going to check out of his hotel and meet her back here for dinner. Tomorrow he wanted to help her hire a bodyguard before she left for Sweden. No time to go to London now. He'd said he wanted to take her to the airport. But what would happen after that? Would she ever see him again?

She was out on the balcony, still drifting in fantasies of a future with Neil when a knock sounded at her door. It was probably Ragi, but Piper still checked the peephole just as Neil had made her promise.

There was no one there.

But on the floor outside the door was another large manila envelope. Her name was written on it in the same hand as the other two. Piper's elation vanished and her insides cramped. How had this nutcase found her?

Slowly, she bent to pick it up. She should just throw it away. Or give it to the police. Who cared what it said?

But as if some invisible force compelled her, she opened it and slid out the note. More cut out letters. Piper read,

If YoU StAy WiTh the seal
yOu wIlL RuIN hiS cAReEr

DO yOu rEAlLY WaNT that?
He May saY he doesn't mInD
buT hE wIlL hATe YOu fOR iT

Piper let the letter float to the carpet. The sandwich they'd grabbed at a drive-through on the way back from the Keys twisted in her stomach. Shaking uncontrollably, she snatched the note up and tore it into pieces.

Who was this sicko? Could all this publicity linking Neil with her really ruin his career? If it did, he *would* hate her. Being a SEAL meant everything to him. It was who he was.

What had she been thinking? They couldn't have a future together. He lived in the States and was gone on missions all the time. She was always traveling for photo shoots, being hounded by reporters. And he couldn't even talk about his missions. He'd never be able to deal with the constant media scrutiny.

She'd been dreaming to think they could make this work.

PIPER'S FLIGHT WAS scheduled for departure in forty minutes.

But Neil wasn't ready to turn her loose.

He scanned the crowds of busy travelers. Several people were staring at Piper. A couple of them had phones out, snapping pictures, filming. This terminal was too public for a last goodbye.

"Give us a minute?" Neil asked Piper's new bodyguard.

The hulk nodded and turned his back, glaring at the

people who had their phones aimed at Piper until they slunk away.

Yeah, he'd do.

Piper spoke into Ragi's ear and the assistant headed down the concourse.

Neil took Piper's elbow and pulled her around the corner behind an eight-foot-tall electronic map of the terminal. This was it. His palms were damp, his mouth dry. He didn't want it to be. But it was the only logical decision. Still, he couldn't make himself say the words. He just stared into her cool green eyes.

"So you like Jim?" he asked as he leaned around the map to catch a glance at the bodyguard.

She shrugged. "You chose him. I trust you."

Neil nodded. "And you'll do as he advises while you're in Sweden? No going off on your own?"

She sighed and rolled her eyes. "I said I would." She folded her arms and refused to look at him.

She'd been acting funny ever since he'd returned to her hotel last night. Not that there'd been a lot of conversation. But still, she'd been…withdrawn.

Although not in bed.

Maybe she'd felt the same sense of urgency that had driven him. She'd been ready the minute he walked through her door. Wearing a hot pink bra and panties set that had his pulse skyrocketing. As he'd kissed her, made love to her, held her after, he had kept thinking this was their last time. He'd never see her again.

Never sleep with her beside him all night. Never see that naughty smile directed only at him. Never hear her say his name.

Afterward, she'd been quiet. Distracted. Maybe she didn't want their relationship to end, either.

But how would something like the two of them even work? He had to get back to Virginia. And her world was an ocean away. Literally and figuratively. He'd been an unlikely fling for her from the beginning.

He took her hand. It was so cold. He rubbed it between his. "Take care of yourself." He winced. Might as well tell her to drive safely, or maybe have a nice life.

She placed her palm on his cheek. "It's been brilliant fun these past few days, Neil." Lifting up onto her toes, she gave him a quick peck on the lips.

Forget that. He grasped her shoulders and opened his mouth over hers, trying to tell her things he had no words for. He wasn't ready for her to leave. Wasn't ready to never see her again.

"How long will you be in Sweden?" He trailed kisses down her neck.

She clung to him. "About a week."

"And after that?" He kissed her ear, her temple, her mouth.

"After that I have a *SportsWorld* swimsuit shoot in Belize." Her fingers combed through the hair at the back of his neck.

"Could you get away for a couple days? I want to see you again."

She pulled back. "What about your career?"

"What about it?" Stroking her long silky hair, he placed tiny kisses on the corners of her full lips.

"Won't the navy mind you being in the public eye because of me?"

She was worried about him? He shook his head, pulling her forehead to his. "No, baby. As long as a mission isn't compromised, I'm good."

Still, she withdrew. Wouldn't meet his gaze. He stilled. Was she looking for an easy way out? "What's all this about?"

She didn't answer.

"If you don't want to see me again, just say so."

Her gaze flew to his, eyes wide. "No! That's not it."

"Then, what is it?" In that moment he knew. "You got another note from him, didn't you? What did it say this time?"

She studied the floor and his blood ran cold.

"Piper. Tell me what it said."

"It said that being with me would ruin you. Your career."

"My career? It specifically mentioned my career?"

"Yes."

Why would Piper's stalker care about that? He was obviously appealing to Piper's conscience, but it almost sounded like the guy was military. Or ex-military. "You gave the letter to the police?"

She bit her lower lip. "I…tore it up."

"Look, the jerk doesn't know what he's talking about. The only thing you have to worry about is, do you want to see me again?" He couldn't believe how much her answer mattered.

The world seemed to light up as she flashed a smile. "I do."

"Then, can you come to Virginia? I know a guy who—"

He felt her chuckle. “You sure know a lot of guys.” She gave him a blistering kiss.

When he came up for air, he finished. “So, this guy I know knows a guy who owns a little B and B out in the middle of nowhere.” He put his mouth on hers, sweeping in with his tongue.

She smiled and then nipped at his bottom lip. “Text me the name of this place your guy knows.”

He grinned against her mouth. “Text me when you can get away.” More kissing—deep, lingering kisses. I-don’t-want-you-to-leave kisses. I-miss-you-already kisses. It was going to be a long month on standby at Little Creek. If he got deployed he’d probably be gone even longer.

“If I can’t make it I’ll let you know, okay?” He framed her face and gritted his teeth. *Just say goodbye, Barrow.*

“Piper.” Ragi’s soft voice.

Neil looked past Piper. Her assistant was hovering, and clearly fretting. “Your flight is boarding.” The hulk was at her side, scowling.

Piper never took her eyes off Neil. “Yes, all right.”

Neil wrapped his arms around her and held her, squeezing her to him for one final moment. “Text me when you get in?”

She nodded against his shoulder, then pushed away and hurried off without looking back.

But damn if her eyes hadn’t been a little damp.

11

Piper was so nervous her hand shook as she knocked on the room door. The little bed-and-breakfast had probably been an old farmhouse at one time. Set in green rolling hills, with plenty of woods and a babbling creek, it was picturesque, but very out of the way. Even with Jim skulking around the premises, it would be more private than a hotel.

Neil had texted that he'd checked in under the name Smith. The lady at the registration desk was polite, giving Piper a conspiratorial smile and a room number.

As if he'd been waiting on the other side, Neil opened the door immediately. He swept her into his arms, devoured her mouth with his and unzipped her dress.

Closing the door behind her, she unbuttoned his jeans and tugged at his zipper.

"Careful." He smiled against her lips. "Not a lot of extra room down there right now."

His chest and feet were bare. His jaw was darkened with evening stubble. "Mmm," she murmured and pressed her palm to his straining erection. "You've missed me?"

"It's been nearly two months." He lifted her dress over her head and then slipped her bra straps off her shoulders and groaned. "I've missed you more than I can ever say. I want to show you how much I've missed you." He opened the front clasp of her bra and the silky material fell to the floor. He mouthed one sensitive nipple and then the other. His hands wandered down her back to cup her bottom and pull her against his hard length.

As he teased and suckled both breasts, Piper leaned against the door and curled one leg around his waist. His dog tags were cold against her skin.

"Well?" Neil raised his brows, waiting.

"Well, what?"

His fingers walked down the front of her knickers and stroked her through the silk. "Did you miss me, too?"

She shut her eyes and moaned his name, the pleasure scorching her. Much more of that and she'd be a goner.

"Tell me you missed me, too."

"Yes," she replied. Her moans were becoming louder, her control slipping.

"Yes, what?" he whispered in her ear.

She could barely think and he wanted words? "Yes, I missed you, too."

He dropped to one knee, sliding her knickers off before bringing his mouth to her hot, wet center.

She was so on edge it took his talented tongue only moments before he sent her flying over it. While she was still trying to catch her breath, Neil tugged off his clothes, rolled on protection and lifted her thigh over his hip. Then, as he held her gaze, he thrust inside her, confident and commanding.

Yes, this! She'd been missing this. Missing him. Not just his spicy cologne or his polite manners or even his powerful body. She missed how he looked at her, as if she was the only one who counted in his world.

He increased the intensity of his thrusts, bumping her against the door again and again. It didn't take long before he was shuddering in her arms, his breathing ragged.

"Welcome to Virginia, ma'am."

"Mmm, are all SEALs so hospitable?"

He grinned, still breathing hard. "We aim to please."

She smiled, one hand caressing his pecs, the other squeezing his cute butt. "Well, you've succeeded."

Her leg slid slowly off him and Neil pressed kisses to her neck. "I already don't want this weekend to end," he mumbled. "I have three more weeks of leave. Let's hole up here." He nipped at her earlobe.

"I can't for that long." Her body was limp, his weight against her. His hands cupping her butt were the only things holding her up.

"Where are you going to be? Maybe I could come there."

She hesitated. Should she tell him what he'd inspired her to do? Her plan to build the orphanage in Delhi was still in its early stages, yet…he knew about Nandan. But unless one had experienced it, no one truly understood the desperate poverty she'd been exposed to. Especially someone like Neil, raised in such privilege.

"Hey, never mind." Reaching for his briefs, Neil stepped away. "I don't want to crowd you."

"No." She realized she'd been silent too long. "I'm going to Delhi." She clasped his arms and played with his dog tags, staring at them. "I go back sometimes, whenever I can."

He covered her hand with his and she looked up into warm, understanding copper-color eyes. "I can respect boundaries."

"That's not it." She swallowed. She wanted to share that part of her life with him. "I'll text you the date and address. Meet me there if you can get the leave, okay?"

"I'll be there." He brought her hand to his lips and kissed the back. "Follow me." With a nod of his head he directed her toward the bathroom.

Piper shed her bra and dropped it on the floor, then joined him. And her breath caught. Dozens of candles lit the bathroom, and the claw-footed tub was filled with steaming water.

"Thought you might want a bath after your long flight." Neil stood in his black boxer-briefs holding a bottle of scented oil.

"Neil, that's so sweet." Her heart melted all over again. She'd been trying to tell herself for weeks now that she'd just been infatuated with a dream guy that existed only in fantasies. That the romantic island location and the stress of the whole situation down in Miami had caused her to be swept away in the moment.

But now all those glorious emotions came rushing back, overwhelming her.

"Climb in." Neil gestured to the tub, skimmed off his briefs and joined her as she stepped in and sank down into the tempting water. With a sigh, she leaned back against him.

She felt him gently brush her hair off her back and pull it over her shoulder to the front and—heaven—he began to massage her nape. "So catch me up. Did you work things out with Cassandra?"

She smiled, amazed he even remembered her quarrel with one of the other Desiree's Desire models, much less cared what had happened. "I did. Thanks to you."

"Me?" His hands rested on her shoulders.

"Don't sound so shocked. Your advice was spot-on. She just needed someone to listen and commiserate with her about the breakup." She toyed with his hand on her shoulder and glanced back at him. "I have a friend now because of you."

He softly kissed her temple. "You have two friends. Remember that."

She closed her eyes and smiled. Yes. She did. She had a friend who made her so happy. A friend who made her a better person. For the first time, she had someone to talk to about anything and everything. Someone to confide in, someone to give her advice.

They'd been texting each other since they'd parted in Miami. Occasionally he'd call, saying he just wanted to hear her voice. The almost three weeks he'd been gone on a deployment, her chest had ached with missing him.

Those had been the longest, most nerve-racking

weeks. Almost as bad as the month she'd spent in India right after she discovered Nandan was missing. Both times she'd had a sick feeling in the pit of her stomach. But Neil had returned.

If only...

"Any word from your PI?"

It was as if he could tell whenever she was thinking of her brother. She shook her head. "No."

He resumed massaging her neck. And if his hands wandered down to play with her breasts, she wasn't going to complain.

In the easy silence, Neil said, "I've been thinking."

"Does it hurt?"

He tickled her ribs and she jerked away and shrieked. "Behave."

"Okay, okay. Thinking about what?"

"Well, I know this guy who—"

"Who knows a guy?" she interrupted.

"Don't make me tickle you again, smart aleck. Yeah, a guy who works in intelligence."

Piper sat up and twisted at the waist to look at him. "Intelligence?"

"Don't get your hopes up, okay? But he said he'd look into your brother's case for me. Do you have a picture of him?"

"Yes. Oh, Neil. I can't believe this. That you would even ask someone..." She turned and straddled him, framed his face and gave him a kiss full of emotions she couldn't begin to name.

"Of course I would ask." He opened his mouth and

returned the kiss—very sensual yet reverent. "I'll need all the info you can give me."

"Oh, yes, whatever you want."

"His full name. The name and address of the family he was staying with."

"Neil, this is amazing." She hugged him and then pressed kisses to his rough jaw, his neck, his collarbone.

They stayed in the tub, kissing and touching, learning each other's bodies until the water was cool and she was so aroused she sank onto his long, hard length.

He groaned, but then grasped her at the waist. "Piper, wait."

She stopped.

"What about protection?"

"I'm on the pill."

"You trust me, then?"

She grinned. She did trust him. "Absolutely."

She rode him until he called out and rested his cheek against her soapy breasts.

Eyes closed, arms tight around her back, he murmured something and mouthed the curve of her breast.

"What?"

He lifted his head and looked deeply into her eyes. "I said, a year ago I wasn't sure I would ever be this happy again."

Funny. Piper wasn't sure she'd ever imagined she would be this happy, period.

That pesky lump was back in her throat.

12

NEIL PAID THE DRIVER and stepped out of the auto-rickshaw, dying of curiosity. The address Piper had given him wasn't some five-star hotel in downtown Delhi. In fact, it wasn't a hotel, as far as he could see.

Glancing around at the crowded squalor, he judged this to be the slum she'd grown up in. He envisioned a young Piper—an orphan—hungry and begging, and closed his eyes. No wonder she'd been willing to leave behind everything she knew to live in a foreign country with a stranger. She'd been determined to make a better life for herself and her brother. Neil could only shake his head in awe at the courage that had taken.

The building he stood in front of was not much more than canvas siding with a corrugated metal roof. But this must be the right place. A sign beside the door read Nandan's House. What was this place?

Neil knocked and waited. Eventually the door was opened by an Indian woman wearing a colorful sari and a warm smile. "Lieutenant! You are welcome. Come in."

She ushered him forward and he was surprised to find the interior cool and clean. The foyer had wooden slats for a floor and was stacked high with plastic tubs. A staircase led to a second floor, and there was a doorway to his left where the woman directed him.

In what he would loosely term an office, Piper sat at a small desk quietly talking with an older man. She looked up and her face lit with a smile he'd missed more than he wanted to admit. "Neil!" Jumping up, she rounded the desk and ran straight into his arms.

Her soft body was draped in a traditional sari, colorful like the other woman's and covering her hair, as well. She looked even more exotic, even more beautiful.

Conscious of the other people in the room, he only pecked her cheek and then stepped back, awaiting introductions.

Mr. Goswami was the business manager and Mrs. Goswami would oversee the place itself.

"It's going to be a children's home," Piper explained. "I thought about what you said, how I ran a corporation. Employed people. And I thought maybe I could do this."

Neil was amazed. Humbled.

"Would you like a tour?" Piper asked, beaming.

"Absolutely." He took the hand she extended and she led him around the dilapidated building as if they were touring the Taj Mahal. The common area behind the staircase was strewn with toys, a TV blared in one corner and an air hockey table sat in the other. There was also a kitchen on the first floor. The second floor was a huge room lined with sleeping pallets, and a few baby beds at one end.

"We will provide school uniforms and supplies, and of course meals." Neil could hear the pride oozing in Piper's voice.

"It's fantastic, Piper." Neil was still holding her hand as they ended the tour. He couldn't explain how close he felt to her right now.

"I'm going to have a grand opening. Invite the media. And everyone I know. I'm going to use my celebrity to solicit donations." She caught his eye. "Will you come?"

He tugged her hand, pulling her close. "I wouldn't miss it." Unless he was on an op.

She studied their entwined hands. "Have you…heard anything from that guy?"

Before they'd left the B and B, Piper had shown him a picture—the only one she had—of her brother and Neil had snapped a pic on his phonc. The photo was small, battered and creased. The boy in it looked to be about six or seven. If Piper had been fifteen when she left India and the boy had been ten, then that would make him about seventeen or eighteen now. But with age-progression technology that shouldn't be a problem.

The guy his buddy had put him in touch with hadn't made any promises. But he'd assured Neil they had an operative who knew the region. If the boy was still alive, the operative might be able to find him, or at least someone who had heard of him. And if the boy wasn't alive? Piper needed to know that, too.

"Nothing yet."

Her shoulders drooped and he could read the anguish in her eyes. She nodded. "Every time I come here," she said softly, still gripping his hand, "I always end up wandering the streets, searching for his face." She shrugged. "I know it's impossible, unlikely. In a city of over twenty-two million, the chances of me spotting him are astronomically small." She looked away from him, watching the children play instead. "I don't even know what he looks like anymore."

Neil slipped an arm around her waist and held her to him, comforting her as she tried to get control of her emotions. After several moments, she drew in a deep breath, wiped her cheeks and stepped back. "I'm so sorry."

He pressed his lips to her forehead. "Don't be."

She glanced at him. "Have you checked into the hotel?"

"I'll do that later. Right now, I want to be with you. And you need to be here. So…" He put his hands on his hips and scanned the plastic tubs full of clothes and food. "Put me to work. I'm yours for the duration." He smiled at her and rolled up imaginary sleeves.

Her grin managed to be joyful and mischievous at the same time. "Mine?" Stepping close, she snaked her arms round his neck. "What if I want you for longer than that?"

13

NEIL STEPPED OUT of the DC metro station and headed for 9th Street. The message had said to meet in front of the International Spy Museum. A little company humor.

The spook hadn't exactly gone through proper channels to obtain his information. But the important thing was, the guy had news.

Neil jingled the keys in his pocket, worrying them like prayer beads. He hoped it was good news.

It'd been a month since he'd seen Piper. Another long, taxing month of missing her and thinking of her as he fell asleep, with only texting, and the occasional moment to Skype to take away the ache. Man, he had it bad.

She was coming to New York next week, though, and he had the weekend off, so they were hoping to meet. If only he could tell her that they'd found her brother.

Once Neil got to the museum he stopped and bent to retie a sneaker—the prearranged signal to identify himself. If he weren't so worried, he'd have gotten a kick out of all this cloak-and-dagger stuff.

"Can you tell me how to get to the National Mall?" The female voice had a distinctive Texas twang.

Neil looked up to see a plump, blonde woman in mom jeans and a T-shirt with a Lone Star flag on the front. She was holding a metro schedule and seemed lost.

"Sure." He straightened and pointed in the direction he'd come. "If you walked from the metro, you just turned the wrong way. Head back to the station and keep going past it."

She seemed confused, so he tried again. "Down at this corner, turn left, go about three blocks—"

"Maybe you could just show me?"

Neil hesitated. He couldn't miss this meeting, but she looked so lost. "Uh…"

"Just messin' with you, hon. Walk with me."

The woman's dazed expression morphed into shrewd intelligence and there was a definite twinkle in her eye. She spun and headed toward the metro station.

Neil blinked and a chill crawled over his skin. He'd met some spies on his missions in Iraq and Afghanistan. But this woman had fooled him completely. He jogged to catch up to her brisk step.

"You want the good news or the bad news first?"

"Uh, the good."

"He's alive."

Neil's shoulders dropped in relief. "And the bad?"

"We think he's in China. In a labor camp."

Neil stopped and closed his eyes. No wonder Piper hadn't been able to find him.

Before he could ask any questions the woman shook his hand, passing off the metro schedule. "Well, thank you so much for helpin' me." Then in a low voice, she said, "Good luck." She strode off, looking around at the buildings like an awe-struck tourist.

Neil waited until he got back to his quarters at Little Creek that evening before he opened the folded, crinkled pamphlet. Out fell a grainy black-and-white photo of a row of young men sitting at a table, all wearing jumpsuits, assembling some sort of electronic equipment. One of the boys had been circled with a black marker. His height—even sitting—and obvious ethnicity made him stand out from the other inmates. On the back of the photo, written in chicken-scratch print, was the name and location of the labor camp.

Neil studied the photo. The boy looked gaunt. At least he was alive. *If* this was Nandan. But the age-progression software was usually accurate. So there was hope. He could tell Piper that.

But how was he going to get the boy out of there?

If an extraction mission failed, it would be a political nightmare of epic proportions. His best hope was to go through diplomatic channels.

Maybe he shouldn't tell Piper until he knew more.

He'd have to talk to someone in the state department. See if there was any way to negotiate the kid's release. But for that to happen he'd have to call in a few favors. Or rather, his father would.

And asking his father for something?

Neil knew there'd be a price to pay.

NEIL PULLED HIS truck under the portico of the River Oak Country Club. The valet scrambled over to take the keys, and when Neil mentioned Senator Patrick Barrow's name, the staff directed him to the sixth hole and provided a golf cart.

He found his father with a couple of other men including—just his luck—Lyndsey's father.

"Neil." His father greeted him with a surprised lift of his brows.

"Sir." Neil shook his hand, and then turned to his father-in-law. "Sam."

Sam scowled, but he shook Neil's hand.

His father coolly introduced him to his other companions. "You remember Congressman Grant, and this is Jed Mahoney."

Another round of handshakes.

"So what brings you here?" His father's eyes gleamed with the satisfying knowledge that he had the upper hand. He knew Neil wouldn't come within ten miles of this icon of elitism unless he wanted something.

"I need to speak with you, sir." Neil took off his dress hat and clasped it under his arm, adopting an at-ease stance. Even though the July day was a steamy ninety-four, he'd come decked out in his service dress, white with all his medals. He was going to need every advantage he could get for this negotiation. And he didn't fool himself into thinking this would be anything less than a delicate game.

Of course, his father made him wait while he pretended to consider whether to speak with his son in the middle of a golf game. It was a strategy Neil knew well.

"Very well." He turned to the other men, excused himself and led Neil away from the green. "Sam has been upset by all this business in Miami."

Ah, the opening hit. Neil ignored the censure. Any reply he gave—whether defensive or apologetic—would be seen as weakness. "I need you to call in a marker with your guy in the state department."

Patrick Barrow came to an abrupt halt and studied Neil closely. "Why?"

"I want someone released from a Chinese labor camp."

His father's eyes widened, but only for a split second. "There's an American citizen being held in a Chinese labor camp?"

"Not American, no."

"Then, I'm afraid it's impossible."

Neil shrugged. "It's been done before." He gazed out over the rolling green hills of the prestigious old golf course as if he didn't really care whether his old man did him the solid or not.

"Not in China."

"Maybe not, but we negotiate on behalf of our allies all the time."

"Yes, but we usually have something or someone the other country wants."

"This kid is an Indian citizen. India is an ally of ours. China wouldn't want the world to know they were holding an Indian citizen against his will."

"Maybe. But why should I use my marker for this?"

Neil met his father's gaze. "To save the life of an innocent young man?"

Patrick looked incredulous. "There are thousands of innocents in camps around the world. Why this one?"

Neil took a deep breath and gambled. "Never mind. I'll find another way." He moved to leave, but his father caught his arm.

"If I do this, I'll need something in return."

Neil hid a smile and faced his father again. "How many?"

Patrick frowned. "How many what?"

"How many cities do you want me to visit with you on the campaign trail in October?"

His father grinned. "Only the major ones. But I want you *and* your wife together. Reconciled."

PIPER ARRIVED AT the bed-and-breakfast before Neil this time. She'd already caught the train from New York when he'd texted he was running late.

The quiet retreat tucked away in the Virginia woods was the perfect way to beat the heat of a Saturday afternoon in August. And the plush bed practically begged for a nap. But she couldn't sleep.

She didn't usually sleep well anyway. Except with Neil, in his arms. The next best thing was talking with him on the phone at night.

After eating dinner alone downstairs, she stepped outside. Piper could hear the creek rushing behind the inn and headed toward the sound.

Jim followed at a discreet distance.

The crickets chirped; an owl hooted somewhere in the twilight. But as she looked around, the isolation suddenly turned ominous. What if that creep was still following her? She hadn't received any more letters from him since that last one in Miami. She and Neil hadn't been seen together publicly since then, so maybe they were safe now.

But what if they weren't?

Even under Jim's watchful eye, the walk wasn't a pleasant idea anymore. She turned around and went back up to the room.

She was drying off after showering when she heard footsteps in the hall outside. There was a soft knock on the door. She almost forgot to check the peephole before she yanked open the door and launched herself into Neil's arms, kissing his face from cheek to cheek and ending with his mouth.

Oh, she'd missed this. His strong presence, his lips moving over hers. Her towel slipped and only his arms around her waist stopped it from falling to the floor. He carried her into the room and kicked the door shut behind him. But he broke the kiss off to stare into her eyes. "I've missed you."

He seemed so serious. She smiled. "I missed you, too."

Frowning, he turned to lock the door.

He seemed distracted, troubled. Maybe he was tired. "Sorry, my dripping hair got you wet." She lifted her arms to wring her hair with the towel and grinned, letting him get an eyeful of her nakedness.

His gaze roamed over her, hungrily, yet with something weird in his expression… Piper froze. "What's wrong?"

He blinked and met her gaze. "I need to tell you something."

An arctic chill slithered over her skin and settled in her chest. Did it have to do with Nandan? It didn't sound good. Had she always known in her heart that he was dead? If that was his news, she didn't want to hear it. She marched to the bathroom and shoved her arms into a robe. Neil didn't follow her or try to stop her or reassure her.

She hesitated, hiding out in the bathroom. Maybe this wasn't about her brother. Maybe Neil was tired of having to sneak around. He was such an honorable guy. This couldn't be easy for him. He was a good man. Whoever had written her those notes was right. Neil was too good for someone like her.

He'd moved to the window, staring out into the darkness.

She braced herself for bad news. "So is this over?"

"What?" He seemed to snap back to their conversation. "No!" He closed the distance between them and folded her into his arms. "No. I'm just— I'm going on a special op, and I don't know how long I'll be gone."

For the first time since he'd walked in, she really looked at him. His smile was weary. There were dark circles under his eyes that hadn't been there the last time she'd seen him. And his jaw was covered in more than simple evening stubble. He was tired—no. Exhausted.

She laid her head on his shoulder. His body was warm and she inhaled the subtle scent of his cologne and…him. "When do you leave?"

"I'm not sure yet."

"But it's something dangerous?"

He shrugged. "Every op has its risks."

Arms wrapped around his waist, she closed her eyes and held on to him. The thought of him risking his life, getting hurt, or worse… She couldn't stand it. But that was his job, wasn't it? The job he loved. If she wanted to be in his life, she needed to get used to it. It wouldn't make things any easier on him for her to act all worried and weepy. She drew in a deep breath. "Something tells me you haven't eaten. Why don't you shower and I'll go bring up some dinner."

His arms squeezed her tight. He tucked his nose into her neck. "I don't want food. I just want you."

She lifted her head away and smiled up at him. "Well, you have me, silly."

An expression of pain flashed across his face, then was gone. "So I do." He smiled.

She stared into his warm brown eyes. Honorable eyes. Kind eyes. Emotion overwhelmed her. She almost blurted out that she loved him. But what if he didn't say it back? Or said it only because he didn't want to hurt her? With a seductive lift of her brow, she stepped away, curled her fingers under his belt and brought him over to the bed. For now, it was enough simply to be with him.

Sitting on the edge, she tugged him between her knees and began unbuttoning his shirt. Something felt different, but the thought passed when he bent and kissed his way down her neck, nudging her robe off her shoulder with gentle fingers. "Piper." His voice sounded strangled.

Missing him desperately already, she covered his

mouth, took the kiss deep and then lay down, pulling him on top of her.

He moaned and pressed his erection against the place she wanted him to be.

Setting to work unbuckling his belt, she raised her head and kissed his chest softly, trailing her mouth over to tease each nipple with her tongue.

Someone rapped on the door.

With a sigh, Neil scrambled from the bed and began buttoning his shirt as he went to answer it. Piper pulled the robe up over her shoulder and adjusted the belt.

She heard the receptionist's voice speaking softly but couldn't understand her words. Neil answered her and then closed the door. He turned to her with a confused expression. "I have to talk to someone downstairs. I'll be right back."

Piper got up from the bed and clutched at her robe. "I didn't think anyone knew you were here."

He scowled and tucked in his shirt. "I didn't, either."

"Do you think it has to do with your mission?"

"Maybe." He ran a hand through his hair. "Just wait here. I'll be right back."

"Make sure Jim is watching for reporters."

He cupped her face and gave her a quick peck on the lips. "I will." Then he was out the door.

Piper waited a few minutes and then another few minutes. Neil didn't return. Patience was not her forte. She quickly got dressed and headed downstairs.

The lobby was empty, but she saw Neil outside on the terrace talking to a woman. Not just talking. Arguing. Neil's fists were clenched at his sides, his body rigid.

Who was this woman? She was tall and slim, her brunette hair cut in a short, stylish bob. Her gray designer suit was impeccable; the pencil skirt fit her slim hips and the hem stopped just above her knees. The expensive shoes alone told Piper that the woman wasn't a reporter.

No way was Piper going to wait obediently in the room now. She opened the door to the B and B and went to Neil's side.

The woman stopped talking and the look she threw Piper was positively venomous.

Piper raised a brow, slipped her hand around Neil's arm and leaned into him. Neil might as well have been made of granite. "Neil, would you like to introduce me?"

The woman's mouth tightened. "I know who you are." Amazing how she could convey such disgust with only a few words.

"Lyndsey." Neil's voice had gone all low, but with a raw edge to it. And he knew the woman's name? Who exactly was she?

"Piper, this is—"

"I'm his wife."

14

"PIPER!"

Neil grabbed her arm as she swayed. Her face had turned ashen.

Piper stared at him. Devastation with a hint of hopeful denial flared in her eyes. "Neil?" She shook her head. "That's not true, is it?" She glanced from him over to Lyndsey and back to him.

"No. Well, not really," he answered.

The glimpse of hope died, her expression hardened. "What do you mean, not really?"

"We *were* married, but—"

"*Are* married," Lyndsey interjected. She wore a satisfied smirk as she held up her left hand and wiggled her ring finger with a large diamond on it.

Piper flinched. "You lied to me, Neil?"

"No, I can explain. Let's go inside. Back to our room."

Piper wrenched out of his grasp and stumbled to one side. She gaped at him as if he were a plague-carrying rodent. "I told you everybody lies, didn't I? I just didn't know how right I was." She spun and scanned the front lawn. "I've got to get out of here."

Neil reached for her again. "Piper. This can all be explained."

She slapped his hand away. "Don't touch me." She tore down the porch steps. "Jim!"

Jim appeared.

"Get the car," she called out. "I'm leaving."

Neil couldn't let her go like this. As Jim headed down the drive, Neil followed Piper.

"Please listen," he pleaded. "It's just a matter of signing the divorce papers, Piper. She won't be my wife anymore."

"Do give it up, darling. You're causing a scene." Lyndsey had in turn followed them from the porch steps.

Piper clamped a hand over her mouth as if she might be sick. Then, gradually, she underwent a transformation. Her shoulders straightened, her eyes lost their bleakness and she focused a cold stare on Lyndsey. "You can have him back. I'm done with him now." She strode off down the drive, her hips swishing as she headed to the waiting car.

Done with him? Not by a long shot. He knew she didn't mean it. Not after what they'd shared. Neil went after her. "Piper! Just listen—"

"Jim, keep him away." Her tone was flat, unemotional; it left him reeling.

Jim blocked Neil while she slipped into the backseat and slammed the door, staring straight ahead.

Neil clenched his fists to keep from knocking the

guard to the ground. But an altercation would only upset Piper more. He'd let her cool off, and then he would explain everything. Besides, Lyndsey was right about one thing. They had caused a scene. He spied a couple sitting on a stone bench situated in a little garden on the grounds. The woman had her phone pointed at Piper.

Wife. The word echoed in Piper's head, but she kept her face a mask of indifference until the car was off the grounds of the B and B. Then her vision blurred, and the lump in her throat began to sting.

Her stomach cramped.

She was going to be sick. But she'd faced worse than this.

The world blurred as tears filled Piper's eyes. What she wouldn't give for a shot of vodka. Or the entire bottle. That was the problem with sobriety. One missed the numbness of inebriation. Booze provided the perfect armor against unwanted emotions.

Her therapist had said that every day she had a choice to make. She could use dangerous substances to dull the bad feelings, or she could face them. With a grim expression, she'd told Piper, "See which one kills you first. In your case, it won't be the bad feelings."

Piper wasn't so sure. Her hands shook and her chest felt so tight she could barely take a breath. She clamped her teeth together but she couldn't stop them chattering. Her lips trembled with the effort to hold it together.

She cursed herself. How could she have been so stupid? But she had no reason to feel betrayed. What had she expected? And why should she care? Why had she thought she could ever trust someone?

Before she got out of the car at Union Station in DC, she wiped her eyes and fixed her makeup.

Since she'd left her purse back at the B and B, Jim paid for her ticket as she made her way down to the train platform. She wished she was back in New York already.

A man stepped into her line of vision.

Neil.

Her face went cold and her heart pounded too fast.

His hair was mussed, as if he'd run his hands through it. His eyes looked sunken and his face drawn. Good. She hoped Lyndsey was giving him hell.

"Can we go somewhere and talk?" he asked.

She set her jaw. "No."

Neil was clenching his teeth, his eyes spitting fire. But at least he kept his voice low. "Then we'll talk here. I haven't lived with my wife in over nine months."

"You misunderstood. I don't want to talk to you, full stop. Jim?" At her raised voice Jim stepped closer, giving Neil a sympathetic shrug.

Neil ignored him. "As far as I knew the divorce was final."

"I don't care." That was a lot nicer than what she wanted to say. She headed farther down the platform, but Neil blocked her path. "Get out of my way."

"Sir, please step back." Jim was easily two inches taller than Neil, but Neil didn't budge.

People were beginning to stare.

"She simply hadn't signed the papers yet, but—"

"I don't want to hear this." She clamped her hands over her ears and squeezed her eyes closed.

Neil grabbed her hands and pulled them away from her ears. "I thought she'd signed the divorce papers."

She didn't want him touching her and yanked her hands out of his grasp. "Even if I cared—which I don't—why should I believe anything you say?"

His eyes narrowed and a muscle in his jaw ticked. "You know what my platoon calls me?" He grimaced. "Straight Arrow Barrow. Like I told you, I don't lie. Ever." He shook his head. "Although I think I've been lying to myself for a while now."

She clicked her tongue in disgust. "I'm not your therapist." Again she tried to move away from him, and again he blocked her path.

"You're right." He spoke through gritted teeth. "If you don't believe me there's nothing I can do to convince you." He paced away from her and came back again, and then met her gaze with eyes blazing. "I won't try to contact you again. But please, don't do anything crazy, okay? I know the real Piper, and she's better than her press releases." Whipping out his mobile phone, he turned and strode for the stairs.

Two long strides. Three. If he thought she was going to call out to him to come back he was delusional.

And what kind of person *never* lied? That was ridiculous. He couldn't expect anyone to believe that.

Besides, even if she did believe him, she wasn't going to call him back anyway.

He was halfway up the stairs. Almost out of her life forever.

Neil!

No. Good riddance. Just because he'd melted her messed-up heart with his talk of honor. Just because he'd understood her like no one else ever had. Just because he was still determined to protect her, even when he thought she hated him.

Then he was gone.

BEFORE PIPER COULD even get back to New York, Ragi called. Social media was buzzing with stories of bad-girl Piper cheating with a married SEAL. Piper was a pariah once again, and there seemed no limit to the nasty comments and name-calling the online world could sling at her. Ragi had contacted Piper's publicist, but there was no saving this mess.

Piper texted Ragi to book the next flight to London and meet her at the airport.

As she and Jim exited the New York train station Piper felt the malicious stares of passersby. Head down, she retreated into a cab and directed the driver to take them straight to the airport.

Ragi was waiting at the terminal with their tickets and a miserable expression.

"Don't look at me like that, Ragi. I didn't know!" In all the time they'd spent together he'd never mentioned having a wife. Or even an ex-wife. She'd assumed he'd been in relationships, of course. He was in his thirties. But married? Stomach still cramping, Piper fought the desire to go into the restroom, close the stall door and hole up for say…the next decade.

Ragi followed her into the security line, eyes downcast. "It is my fault. Because he is a member of the special forces, his personal information is not a matter of public record. Still, I should have discovered the lieutenant had a wife. I offer you my resignation."

"No, Ragi. I can't lose you now. We'll…weather this somehow."

After a moment's hesitation, Ragi nodded and returned her attention to her phone, thumbs racing.

By the time the plane touched down in London, the British rags sported headlines like Homewrecker Strikes Again! and SEAL's Wife Catches Bad-Girl Piper in the Act!

As they took a cab to Piper's flat, Ragi mumbled, "Oh, no."

Piper glanced over at her friend and assistant. Ragi had clicked on her phone with her thumb, scrolled down once and then looked up with devastation in her eyes. That could only mean one thing.

"Modelle?"

Ragi's face went slack as she nodded. "They will not be renewing your contract."

The twisting in Piper's stomach was relentless, but it wasn't from pain anymore. She'd done nothing wrong! Nothing intentionally. She wanted to open her mouth and shriek. She wanted to throw something, pound her fists into the back of the seat in front of her. Not getting this contract might only be the beginning. Others could also decide she was too volatile to use. She could lose everything.

As it was, without the extra income from the makeup company, she'd have to give up the flat in London. The posh flat she'd hoped she would one day share with Nandan. To give him the life she'd promised him when she left.

But she could always find a less lavish flat. What she couldn't do was give up the private investigators or the children's home in Delhi.

When she stepped out of the cab, paparazzi swarmed her. She summoned her courage. If she'd already been condemned, it wouldn't matter what she said. Her hands shook. Why had she bothered to change her life? What good had being good done her?

And why should she slink into her flat with her tail between her legs? She smiled and posed while cameras flashed. Jim hovered while Ragi paid the driver and saw to the luggage.

"Piper, is the SEAL going back to his wife?"

She held up her hands and shrugged. "How should I know?"

"So you and the SEAL have broken up?"

She faked a yawn. "I was bored."

"Piper, what about the baby?"

Baby? Piper blinked, a montage flashing before her of her being pregnant and Neil's hand feeling the baby kick, lying in a hospital bed holding an infant and Neil smiling down at both of them. Neil helping a toddler walk…

Rubbish! She scrubbed those pictures from her mind and focused on the reporter who'd asked. "There is no baby," she replied. Then she glanced at Jim and he cleared a path so she could get into her building.

Once inside her flat—Jim stationed outside her door—she strode to her bedroom. Ragi hurried to follow. "Piper, what should we—"

"You can have the next week off, Ragi."

"But—"

"Ragi!" Piper clamped her mouth shut. Ragi was only trying to help. "I'll be fine. Take some time off, Ragi, all right?"

After Ragi left, Piper showered and crawled into bed. As if she would sleep. Neil! How could he have lied to her? Was that why he'd been acting so funny when he arrived at the B and B? Maybe he didn't really have to leave on a mission? Maybe nothing he'd ever told her had been true.

It hurt to think he'd been lying all this time. All she could picture was his easy smile. His touch. His mouth. His…everything.

It suddenly hit her. Last night when she'd unbuttoned his shirt—his dog tags had been missing.

TWELVE HOURS LATER, Piper left the flat in her skimpiest dress, her highest stilettos and too much makeup. She exited the lift and entered the lobby hoping there were plenty of paparazzi outside to snap her photo before she got in a cab.

For the next week, she made sure to be seen at all

the clubs. She drank. She danced. She did what everyone expected bad-girl Piper to do.

Until she read another tabloid headline that stopped her in her tracks.

Navy SEAL Resigns Amid Rumors of Court Martial Over Extramarital Affair!

15

NEIL COULDN'T FEEL his fingers anymore.

Gluing grass and twigs onto his camouflage ghillie suit had required bare hands. His nose had lost any sense of feeling days ago. His toes would be next. But lying completely still on his stomach in cold, wet grass for over a week had hardened him to most everything.

Except for the look on Piper's face at the B and B. *That* he saw day and night, waking, sleeping.

He tried not to think about it, but observing the routines of a labor camp, the guards' movements and any traffic coming and going still left a lot of free time over the course of a week.

At first, he'd been too busy planning the extraction. Clay had helped. Even offered to go with him. But no way would Neil let Clay ruin his career, much less risk his life when the odds of making this crazy scheme work were so small.

This covert op was strictly off the books. If the Chinese authorities discovered what he was doing there'd be international repercussions. And that would be the least of his troubles.

The government would never have sanctioned an extraction op for someone who wasn't an American citizen. So Neil had tendered his resignation. He couldn't explain it to Clay. He barely understood it himself. He just felt in his gut this was something he had to do.

He'd left some letters with Clay in case things went badly. One for his mother. One for Piper.

The only movement he made now was to slowly lift the binoculars to his eyes and watch, then record the camp's activities into his notebook. Every guard, every shift change, every time the prisoners were allowed outside. Hour after hour…

After landing in Delhi, he'd pored over maps of the area, researched routes and scouted possible points of entry and exit. It turned out the border between China and India had had some trouble recently with the Chinese army encroaching and the Indian army setting up a watchtower in the area. That had made sneaking in a bit more difficult.

In the end he'd gone across on foot on a dark, moonless night, carrying everything he needed on his back over the mountainous terrain. The labor camp lay at the base of the Himalayas. Just getting here had taken five days. And who knew what condition Nandan would be in? Neil had to allow a couple of weeks for the return journey. He could only be grateful it was summer.

And that he'd decided not to tell Piper. She'd have wanted to go with him. And he couldn't have risked that. Plus, what if he failed? What if he and Nandan were killed during the escape? Neil had risked his own life countless times. But he couldn't raise her hopes like that only to have them snatched away.

Maybe it was better that she hated him. But hurting her—even unintentionally—had just about torn his heart out. Coward that he was, he'd almost blurted out everything on the metro platform. About the bargain he'd tried to make with his father. About his decision to resign from the navy and try to rescue Nandan. How much he loved her. How he didn't want to hurt her. Ever. How much he wanted a life with her.

But he couldn't say any of that. She might've tried to talk him out of going after her brother. Or she might not have. He didn't want to know which. Better she get on with her life without him. She still had so much living to do. Once she had her brother with her, she'd barely remember her brief affair with a navy SEAL.

And she did hate him. She'd let him walk away without listening to his explanation. He wished he knew what she'd been thinking. Cursing him? Probably.

But he was going to remember her for the rest of his life. The way she'd looked that last night together at the bed-and-breakfast. He'd smelled her soft citrus shampoo, seen her light green eyes sparkling with passion. And when she'd dropped that towel? He'd had to clench his fists to keep from taking her right then.

He dreamed of her like that, night after night.

His stomach turned just thinking about the deal his father had offered. The devil himself couldn't have come up with a more soul-shredding pact.

Neil had flatly refused. Even the appearance of reconciliation with his ex would be a betrayal of everything he believed in.

He hadn't spoken with Lyndsey since she'd surprised them at the B and B. That could wait until he got back from this mission.

If he made it back.

Powder-blue jumpsuits drew Neil's attention to the courtyard of the labor camp. Prisoners were pouring out of the side door of what Neil had determined must be the work building. Right on time, the prisoners were marched outside to sit in rows on the ground and eat their one bowl of rice.

Neil could always spot Nandan without too much trouble. He was at least half a foot taller than most of the other inmates. Tall, like his sister. Apart from being malnourished, the boy looked fairly healthy. And he had youth on his side. He should be able to make the trek to the border.

After exactly thirty minutes, the prisoners filed back to their sleeping quarters on the east side. Neil had been creeping closer and closer in the same direction, inch by inch every hour, every day until he was as near as he dared get in daylight.

There were surveillance towers on each corner, and the guards were mercilessly punctual when it came to shift changes, meal times and radio checks. One guard in particular was young and cocky with a nicotine addiction and a tiny bladder. He was Neil's best hope.

Tonight would be the night. Once it got dark he repainted his face in black instead of green, slipped out of his ghillie suit and checked his belt for the pocket-size bolt cutters and his tranquilizer gun. The fence had barbed-wire coiled along the top, but the chain-link fence below could be easily cut. He wouldn't be able to leave so much as a shell casing to identify himself as the intruder, so a tranq would have to do if he got stopped.

Even if this mission was a success, the fallout could still be disastrous. Only two things might save his butt. The fact that China wouldn't want to publicly admit that someone had been able to escape one of their "reeducation facilities," and that if they did suspect any US involvement, they wouldn't be able to prove it.

The young guard arrived for his shift at exactly midnight as usual. And by 2:00 a.m. he'd climbed down from his tower.

Neil moved fast, cut the chain-link fence, crawled through and raced for the prisoners' sleeping quarters. He checked on the guard, who was headed for the corner of the fence shadowed by the tower. Neil knew he would soon be occupied with lighting a cigarette and then relieving himself.

No guard was stationed at the prisoners' sleeping quarters, but the door was latched from the outside. He could only hope no one noticed the latch was open after he entered. But in all his time watching the camp, no guard had ever checked this door at night.

Next came the hard part. Finding the boy among the dozens of blanket-covered cots. Neil switched to his night-vision goggles and scanned the rows of beds for feet sticking over the end.

Row after row and no luck. A momentary panic hit his gut. What if… There! A pair of long, lanky legs and big, bare feet. Silently, Neil moved to the head of the cot. It was him. Nandan.

He clamped a hand over the boy's mouth and the kid jerked awake. Neil held a finger over his lips and then said in a low voice into the boy's ear, "Anju sent me to get you out."

The boy's eyes widened.

"Get dressed. Come with me."

When the boy nodded his understanding, Neil slowly removed his hand from the kid's mouth.

While the boy dressed, Neil opened the door a crack and checked the guard's location. He was back in the tower. But Neil knew he would leave his post once more during his shift. They'd wait him out.

Signaling for the boy to stay in his cot, Neil kept watch at the door with his tranq gun drawn. Finally, after what seemed like an eternity, but in fact was only a couple of hours, the guard left the tower for the shadowed corner again. The boy had fallen asleep. Neil woke him with a hand over his mouth and motioned for him to follow. Now out the door, relatch it and sprint across the courtyard to the tall grass where he'd cut the fence.

Neil's heart was racing. Then he heard a shout behind them.

In one motion, Neil turned and shot the guard running after them. Before the man had even dropped to the dirt, Neil was shoving Nandan through the opening he'd cut in the chain link and urging him to run across the wet grass.

Neil sprinted over to the unconscious guard, retrieved the tranq dart and then positioned the man to look as though he'd fallen asleep at his post. Heart pounding, he raced back to the fence, crawled through and caught up to the kid, guiding him toward an outcropping of boulders two clicks away.

He'd set up a camp of sorts and hidden his gear and equipment there. He'd brought a set of thermals for Nandan, along with food, water…everything they'd need for the long journey back.

But after about half the distance, Nandan was falling behind, too weak to run the full distance.

Neil bent, hefted the kid up and over his shoulders and ran like hell.

IT WAS POURING again tonight. Piper curled up on the window seat in her bedroom, staring out at the sheets of rain drenching everything in sight. Colors dulled. People drooped. Hopelessness was like a fever in her blood.

It rained a lot in London, but so many days of ominous dark clouds weighed on her psyche, suffocating her.

Considering she'd decided to be Britain's number one bad girl again, she'd been staying home a lot lately. Partying the night away only made her feel emptier. Besides, she had a shooting assignment in a couple of days and she wanted to pack up the flat and get it on the market. She was hardly ever here anyway. Maybe she'd buy something small outside the city.

She sighed and wrapped her arms around her bent knees tucked under her chin.

The creep who'd sent her the letters in Miami had been right after all. She had ruined Neil's career. Unwittingly. But even though she tried to tell herself he'd gotten his just desserts by having to resign from the navy, she couldn't help but feel that if only they'd never met, or if only she'd refused his dinner invitation that first night, none of this would've happened. He would still be a SEAL and she'd have her Modelle contract.

Piper pressed her palms to her eyes. *Stop it.* Crying was weak and useless. So were "if onlys." And as much as she tried to convince herself that she hated him, she didn't. And the worst of it was that even knowing how things would turn out, she would do the same thing all over again. She rubbed at the ache in her chest. She missed him so much. His smile. His kiss. How he'd made her feel—as if she could do anything.

Her mobile chimed. Expecting Ragi, she checked the ID. The investigators she'd hired? She clicked Answer. "Hello?"

"Ms. Piper?"

"Yes, what is it? Didn't you receive your last payment?"

"Yes, ma'am. That's not why we're calling. We have some good news."

There was a pause and Piper sat up, afraid to hope, the moment feeling surreal.

"We've found your brother."

16

"THIS IS MESSED UP, MAN." Clay practically spat the words. "She should know what you did for her."

"Let it go, Bellamy." Neil ducked farther behind the corner of the Delhi hospital just as Piper pushed open the door and stepped outside with her brother. Even in the monsoon-like rain she looked radiant.

Neil peered around the edge of the building, watching with an aching heart as she guided her brother toward the limo.

She was as beautiful as ever. Two months. Two of the longest months of his life since he'd seen her. Neil gripped the handles on his crutches until his knuckles turned white. The torn ligament in his knee was nothing compared to the pain of seeing her up close without being able to hold her one last time.

She was focused only on Nandan, her arm wrapped tightly around him, smiling, talking. Seconds before the boy got into the car, she threw her arms around him and squeezed him tightly to her. The look on her face—Neil would never forget the joy.

As if he wasn't accustomed to hugs, the boy just stood there. Eventually, his face crumpled and he put his arms around his sister. She started reassuring the boy about getting him a visa and bringing him to live with her in London, then she was brushing the hair off his forehead and hugging him some more. Her eyes shone with happiness. Neil felt a spasm of jealousy. He wanted to celebrate with her. Have her smile at him like that.

After the limo pulled away, Neil swung his crutches toward the waiting auto-rickshaw and Clay followed him.

"So the Delhi investigators get all the glory?" Clay shook his head. "Like I said, it ain't right."

Neil shrugged. "That was the deal. They get credit for finding the kid as long as they let me know when Piper was arriving to pick him up."

"I should've resigned and come with you. Look at your nose all frostbitten. I can't let you go anywhere on your own."

Neil smiled. He knew Clay was trying to ease the ache. "And have to carry you over the mountains, too?"

Clay snorted. "Yeah, right. I'd have been carrying *you*."

"With your bad back? I don't think so."

Clay sighed. "Neither of us is getting any younger. But you threw away fourteen years of service. Another six and you could've retired with your pension."

"But another six years of what? We both know our ops days are limited." He clapped Clay on the shoulder. "Come on, Bellamy. It's not unheard of for SEALs to get out by the time they're our age."

Clay turned his back to Neil, kicked a rock. "Don't think I don't know."

Neil stopped at the auto-rickshaw and tried to ignore the knot of emotion lodged in his throat. He prayed Piper would be happy. That she would find a good man someday, a man who saw in her what Neil had seen. That the bad-girl act was exactly that. An act.

Clay climbed into the auto-rickshaw. "You sure you should've checked yourself out, Barrow?"

Neil nodded. "Let's get out of here." He handed Clay his crutches and swung himself into the seat beside him. Now he could go home. Not that he had a home. But he was ready to get out of this country and back to the States.

He still had one more thing to take care of before he could start his new life.

NEIL'S STOMACH TURNED as he pulled into the driveway at Lyndsey's house. The colorful autumn foliage lining the suburban street gave the Virginia home a postcard-perfect quality that belied the truth. Once, there'd been a lifetime of dreams associated with its purchase. But now it only represented failure. Or maybe stupidity.

Her car wasn't parked out front. He sighed. Late as usual. At one time he'd thought her insane schedule would mesh well with his constant deployments. Ultimately, it had meant that they never saw each other. Not her fault any more than his. But it was a rare relationship that could withstand that much time apart.

Finding the spare key under the pot of marigolds on the front porch, he let himself in. He'd asked her to meet him here so they could finally have that talk she'd wanted two and a half months ago.

Using the cane to lean on, he headed straight for the study, the divorce papers he'd brought rustling in his suit coat pocket like a caged bird fluttering to be free.

Looking around, he saw Lyndsey hadn't changed a thing. This room had been meant to be his office. Though Lyndsey had decorated and furnished the whole thing. The wall of bookshelves with hardcovers of best-sellers neither of them had read, the mahogany desk and chair she'd bought him for his birthday that he'd never used.

He'd never been a sit-behind-a-desk kind of guy. But, he'd since realized, she'd thought she could make him into that man. Or maybe she'd just never really known him.

He hobbled to the shelves, ignoring the shooting pains in his torn knee. There were a few books about navy SEALs he'd left behind. Maybe he'd take those. He glanced at his watch. How much longer would he have to wait? He wasn't leaving without her signature even if he had to hang around here all night.

Irritated, he moved over to the desk for a pen so he could say his piece, have her sign the papers and then get the heck out of there. He yanked open the main drawer. And froze.

Slowly he reached in and pulled out a piece of printer paper. It had letters cut from a magazine that were glued onto the page. The message was a warning to Piper to stay away from him. Exactly as Piper had described the threats she'd received.

What the—?

The front door opened and slammed shut. "Neil?"

Lyndsey.

Shaking with fury, Neil limped to the window overlooking the neatly landscaped yard. "In here."

Lyndsey's heels clicked on the foyer's expensive tile.

He was still holding the stalker letter when she appeared in the doorway. "I'm so glad you called, dear. I thought maybe we'd have some dinn—"

Neil swung around to face her, holding up the letter. "Why?"

She paled, but recovered quickly. "What is that?"

"Don't." He shook his head. "Just…don't. What was the plan here?"

Her mouth tightened. She drew in a deep breath and sauntered over to the desk. "Plan? What are you talking about? I've never seen that before."

"Lyndsey. You'll never make your living on the stage. Drop the innocent act."

Her face twisted into a sneer. "I had you fooled for quite a while, as I recall."

Neil felt nauseated. Who was this bitter woman? What had happened to his childhood friend? Or had she only existed in his mind? "Probably not something you want to brag about, hon. Not to a man with nothing left to lose."

"What do you mean?" she asked.

"Explain this note now, or I swear I'll call the police and let you explain it to them."

She seemed startled. "I knew when I saw your picture in that tabloid with her that she would ruin you. And I was right. Look what happened."

"Thanks to *you*!" Neil slammed the note on the desk. "You refused to sign the divorce papers, and then you show up at that B and B where Piper and I were and ruin—"

"You shouldn't have been there with her!" Lyndsey yelled. She never yelled. But her eyes had a wild look to them. Almost unbalanced. But would someone who wasn't unbalanced send letters like this?

"Were you there? In Miami?"

She scoffed. "Certainly not. Your father said he knew someone. He helped me arrange it. He was as eager as I was to get that tramp away from you."

Neil fought the urge to argue with her. After all, it wouldn't do any good. It wouldn't undo any of the horrible damage she'd caused.

And, of course, there was his father. Neil should've known. He grabbed the papers out of his pocket and dropped them on the desk. "I want you to sign these right now."

She huffed. "Neil, you can't—"

"Right now or I go to the police."

She gave a condescending little smile. "It'd be my word against yours."

"And in the meantime, your name gets dragged through the mud. I doubt your lobbying firm would like that."

Her eyes narrowed and she practically snarled. "Fine." She strode over, grabbed the pen he handed her and flipped through the pages, scratching her signature over and over.

Every time she signed her name Neil felt another weight lift off his chest.

When she finished, she pitched the pen across the desk.

He snatched up the papers and strode out of the room as quickly as someone using a cane could. After his lawyer filed this document with the court, Neil would be his own man again.

"Neil…" Lyndsey called after him as he got to the door.

Only because they'd once been friends, he stopped.

"You would've come back to me if you hadn't met her."

He glanced over his shoulder, his hand moving for the doorknob. "That was never going to happen."

17

Piper stood in the rain, drenched, but not cold. The air was hot and humid. She knew she was in Delhi, but she had no idea how'd she'd gotten here. She was searching for Nandan. But she didn't know what he looked like, so she stood in the middle of the street calling his name.

Then he appeared out of the shrouded mist. Her brother, all grown up! Tall and lanky. Too skinny. A stranger. But not a stranger. Oh, Nandan.

She ran to him, but he disappeared down an alleyway. Piper raced after him. When she turned the corner into the alley, a man stood in the shadows. Not Nandan.

She approached him with caution. As she drew closer, his face became clear.

Neil.

Huddled from the rain. Bedraggled. Weary.

His face so dear. Neil. Her love. Her honorable betrayer. Piper's heart ached. Her tears mixed with the rain. She wanted to run to him and throw her arms around him. But she couldn't move.

Neil's gaze penetrated her soul. His dark eyes seemed to say that everything would be okay and that she should be happy. She was deliriously happy, and yet frozen with grief. Then he gave her a weak salute and strode away from her down the alley.

She wanted to cry out to him not to go, but she couldn't speak. All she could do was watch helplessly as he rounded the corner and was gone forever.

Piper awoke with a shout.

Then she burst into tears. She grabbed up a pillow and muffled her sobs so Nandan wouldn't hear them.

She'd almost contacted Neil so many times. After Nandan went to bed at night, she'd be on the sofa with her mobile, her finger poised over the call button. But she had her pride. She'd given him her complete trust. And he couldn't even tell her he'd been married.

The mind was a funny thing. It had the capacity to make you believe something simply because you wanted it desperately to be true.

She'd actually imagined for a short time that Neil loved her. He'd never said the words. Certainly, the passion between them had been real enough. But he was an important man, the son of a powerful politician, a war hero in his own right. And she posed for magazines in underwear and partied with shallow sycophants and self-important billionaires. What could he have seen in her besides a fun time for a short while?

But it hadn't felt that way.

By the time the sun rose, Piper had been to the shop for scones and eggs and coffee.

She crept into Nandan's room. *"Śubha prabhāta."*

She greeted him in Hindi, but Nandan had heard and spoken nothing but another language for at least five years. Not that he spoke much at all now. She bent to brush the hair off his forehead. “Nandan.”

He barely stirred.

Worried, she opened the curtains on a sunny morning. “Nandan, wouldn’t you like to get some new clothes today?”

He lifted his head and then turned his back to her, burrowing under the covers.

It’d been almost two weeks since she’d returned to London with him and he’d barely left his bedroom. At first, she’d understood his wish to do nothing but sleep and eat. So she’d brought home some new clothes and shoes. But it seemed as if he wanted to hide from the world.

The private investigators would only say that he’d escaped from a Chinese labor camp. Even after three days in the hospital in Delhi, Nandan was still suffering from malnutrition. The frostbite on his fingertips and toes was finally healing, but she hadn’t had the courage to ask about the years he’d been separated from her. She wasn’t sure he would ever talk about it.

She kept picturing her little brother in that horrible camp. Imprisoned. Isolated. Had he been beaten? How had he gotten there? What had happened? She wanted that family she’d entrusted him with to pay for not taking care of him as they should’ve.

Every time she’d suggested to Nandan to go out the past few days, he’d pulled his irritated face. On one hand, she loved that exasperated expression, such a typically teenage thing to do. On the other hand, she couldn't allow him to bury himself away in the flat forever.

"Please, Nandan. Come with me today. The sun is shining. The shoes I bought you don't really fit. You need to try them on. And I thought we'd get you your own phone and maybe a computer to play games on."

He lifted his head. "Games?"

Hope filled her. Maybe that was the key. He loved playing games on her phone. Day and night he plagued her to bring up games for him and played until her battery was drained.

"Yes, but you have to use it for school, too," she said in Hindi. Then she switched to English. "Okay?" She held her breath and waited while he seemed to be considering it.

"Okay." He grinned and climbed out of bed.

Piper breathed a sigh of relief and gave him a brilliant smile. *"Jaldī sē pōśāka."* She shooed him toward his closet. "Dress quickly."

As soon as he ate, they set off for the shops. Jim flagged them a taxi and as they climbed in, a couple of determined reporters asked who Nandan was. Piper wrapped her arm around him and refused to comment.

Once they were in the cab, he craned his neck to see everything, especially Big Ben and the London Eye.

"Would you like to ride the Ferris wheel, Nandan?"

He turned wary eyes on her. "Is it safe?"

"It's very safe. Though maybe we can wait for another day, okay?"

He nodded and then smiled. "Okay."

Once they entered the computer shop, he really lit up as he tried everything, asking questions. He was so happy, Piper spent way too much buying him several gaming systems with all the accessories.

At lunch, Jim hovered at a table close by and a few people snapped photos on their mobiles, but mostly she and Nandan had their privacy. Her brother ordered enough for two and managed to eat every bite. As a kid, she remembered him as a little chatterbox. Always telling her about the things he'd learned in school. But now, as if interacting at the shop had exhausted all his social skills, he asked her to bring up a game on her phone and became completely absorbed in it. Next stop was a mobile phone shop.

Nandan jumped when her phone rang. He touched the screen, and it rang again.

Piper checked the ID. "Nandan, Ragi is calling me. I need to talk to her." She held her hand out, expecting the phone.

He scowled. "I can do it." He started clicking on every button until the mobile stopped ringing. Piper frowned. Now she'd have to call Ragi back, and Ragi's phone would be busy while she left Piper a message and—

"That's Neil."

Piper was sure her heart had stopped. To hear that name coming from her brother's mouth. "What?"

Nandan pointed at her phone.

Piper leaned across the café table to look at the screen.

It was the picture of Neil lying on the hammock in Key Largo.

She couldn't breathe.

The café, the street, the world wavered and split apart. Piper opened her mouth but no sound came out.

"Anju?" She felt Nandan's hand gripping hers where it rested on the table.

His worried face came into focus. She dragged in a deep breath. "How do you know him?" Piper pointed to the picture of Neil.

"Vaha āpa kō mujhē ghara lē āyā." Nandan's face brightened. "He brought me home to you. I want to see him, Anju." Animated for the first time, Nandan talked about his escape from the camp. In Hindi, he told her how Neil had cut the fence, sneaked in, subdued the guard. How they'd traveled for days and days, that Neil had given him boots and socks and kept watch out in the cold while Nandan slept in the warm tent. How Neil had carried Nandan when he couldn't walk another step. "He was injured. Because of me. I wish to thank him, Anju."

Piper could hardly comprehend what Nandan was saying. Neil? Neil had snuck into China and… *He* had been the one to rescue her brother?

Nandan growled low in his throat. "I forgot."

"Forgot what, *Māśūqa*?"

"I wasn't supposed to tell."

She felt dizzy. "Wasn't supposed to tell what, Nandan?"

Anguish wreathing his face, he gripped her arm.

"Neil said he would get into trouble. Surely it was permissible to tell you, was it not, Anju?"

Piper rubbed his arm, soothing him. "It's okay, Nandan. Yes, it's permissible. He won't get into trouble." She came up out of her chair, crouched down next to her brother and put her arm around his shoulders. "You said he was hurt, Nandan? How was he hurt? Is he okay?"

"He fell a long way and after that he limped."

Tears streamed down her face. Neil. The things she'd said to him. How she'd treated him. And he'd done all this? Risked his life? If he'd been caught, the Chinese would've locked him up and thrown away the key. Or worse. She went numb with fear.

Her brother's eyes were filled with tears. "So he is a friend, Anju? You can call him?" Nandan offered her mobile back to her. "Tell him I want to thank him. Learn if he is not hurt anymore."

She looked at her phone in Nandan's hand. Call Neil? A polite thank-you over the phone? She wanted to dash out into the street and flag down a taxi and run to him. Beg his forgiveness for her petty insecurities.

A sick feeling hit her. She fell back into her chair. Even if she could get on a plane this very second, she didn't know where he lived. He'd once mentioned an apartment on the military base where he was stationed. But he wasn't part of the navy anymore.

Her heart stuttered. Those missing dog tags. She'd noticed them gone before the scandal hit the papers. Certainly, he hadn't… He'd rescued her brother. And he'd used the private investigators to hide that from her. She hadn't known. What else didn't she know?

Oh, Neil. What did you do?

He'd sacrificed his career. And it was her fault. But she had her brother back. Would she have told him not to go if she'd known what he'd planned?

Now she didn't even know if Neil was okay. What kind of injuries had he sustained? She had to find him. She had to go to him. She reached for her mobile.

But would Neil want to see her? Would her appearance only disrupt his life again? What if someone put two and two together and did get Neil into trouble for rescuing her brother?

Maybe the best thing she could do for Neil was to stay out of his life. Hadn't he risked enough for her?

And why would he have done that if he didn't care for her? She sat silently, her thoughts jumbled, everything she felt, all the events of the past few months twisted into a giant bundle of indecision.

"You all right, ma'am?"

Jim stood over her.

For Nandan, she had to pretend everything was okay. Had to wipe her face, make herself smile up at the man. "Yes. I'm fine." In a daze, Piper stood, pointing to her mobile still in Nandan's hand. "You can call him." She spoke in Hindi. "When we get home. You can tell him thank you."

That would be best for everyone.

Right?

Neil didn't want to hear from her. Piper closed her

eyes, remembering the last thing he'd said to her. *I won't try to contact you again.* He would honor his word.

Of course, he'd also told her not to do anything crazy…

18

What was he doing here?

Neil questioned his actions—and his sanity—for the umpteenth time in as many days.

But it was too late now.

Actually, it'd been too late the minute he'd opened the invitation to this billionaire's shindig.

When the cab rolled to a stop at the gated entrance to a cliff-side villa in the south of France, Neil showed his invitation and ID to the armed security officer inside the guardhouse and was waved on through.

Limos lined the drive that wound along the grounds, so Neil paid the cabbie, climbed out and walked the rest of the way. He winced at the twinge in his knee, but he refused to let anybody see him limp up to the front doors.

Another guard checked his ID before letting him inside and, as he wandered through the gathering of the presumably rich and fabulous, he noted the security cameras in the corners of each gilded room and the dozens of trained personnel stationed along the walls. Good. This French financier guy better have the best security money could buy given that Piper was here. Lyndsey wouldn't have harmed Piper, but that didn't mean other disturbed folks with a lingerie obsession weren't out there.

He entered a huge ballroom lit with chandeliers and featuring artwork that probably cost more than his entire net worth. At one end, an orchestra played a Sinatra tune. Tugging at his bow tie, Neil spied a bar set up along one wall and headed that way.

As he sipped the excellent scotch, he tried to remind himself that his personal check to Nandan's House—and the one he'd convinced his mother to write—would help kids in need, and that that was the most important thing tonight.

That and glimpsing Piper.

Neil took another sip of his drink and scanned the crowd. Jewels sparkled, champagne bubbled, men in tuxes mingled. But he didn't see Piper.

Just as well. He probably shouldn't have come. It would only break his heart all over again to see her after all these months.

He'd finally gotten his life to where he had mostly good days. He had his cottage in the Keys. He had his boat. He had his job checking security systems for the rich mansions in South Beach. He was…content.

He stilled with his drink halfway to his mouth.

She wore a long strapless gown that was a shade of purple he would now always think of as Pleasurable Plum. Her long black hair was swept up in one of those fancy but messy hairdos that looked as if she'd just twisted it up with a couple of pins. Her bangs and a few wispy strands framed her lovely face. Neil wanted to bury his fingers in her silky hair and tumble it down. She wore dark red lipstick, but no jewels. She didn't need them. Her smile was enough to light her face.

She was talking excitedly with a group of people he didn't recognize. Not that he would know anybody here. He let out a relieved breath. She looked happy. Then he frowned. He didn't see Jim anywhere near her. Why wasn't her bodyguard close by?

He double-checked, but no Jim.

She wouldn't have gotten rid of him, would she? Surely she knew, even if she hadn't received any more letters from his ex, that she should keep a bodyguard full-time.

As Neil kept watch, a tall, dark-haired man stepped close to her side and whispered into her ear. Piper angled her head as the guy slipped his hands possessively around her waist.

Neil clenched his fists. The man's touch was just a little too proprietary.

Piper smiled at whatever Mr. Hands was saying and nodded.

And then she spied Neil. Her smile faded quickly.

Neil almost turned and left. But he rejected the idea flat-out. He wouldn't slink off. He was so hungry for her he'd take her anger if that was all she had to give him.

As he headed toward her, the crowd dissolved and the only person he saw was her.

Her expression was unreadable. But how she was staring at him… So intense.

He stopped a couple of feet away.

"You came." She sounded breathless. Was that from the other guy's touch? He noticed her bare throat work to swallow and his pulse sped up.

He licked his dry lips, remembering the trip to Delhi and the week they'd spent working at the orphanage in the exhausting heat and how he'd promised to come if she held a charity event. "I told you I wouldn't miss it."

Mr. Hands nodded at Neil. "Is this him?"

"*Oui*, Francois. This is Lieutenant Neil Barrow. Neil, this is your host, Francois Giroux."

The Frenchman extended his right hand. "Thank you for coming."

Obviously, the guy would have a French accent. Why was a French accent such a turn-on for women? Neil shook the man's hand.

Mr. Hands gave him an assessing look. "Piper has spoken of you, of course."

"Really? She never mentioned you."

The Frenchman chuckled. "I see what you mean, *cherie*." He spoke to Piper, his hand still resting on her hip, but he kept his gaze on Neil. He leaned down to speak in her ear. "Very American."

Piper smiled, reached up to caress his cheek and gave him a quick kiss.

Neil wanted to punch the guy.

Mr. Hands bowed curtly, turned on his heel and sauntered off.

"What's that supposed to mean? *Very American*."

Neil tried to copy the French accent and failed miserably. He recognized his bitterness for what it was. Envy. Not for the Frenchman's possessions, but because this world, Francois's world, was where Piper belonged.

Though he sure didn't want to live in this world. He'd joined the navy to get away from it. Like a neon sign flashing in front of his eyes, it hit him hard that she didn't belong in a tiny cottage in the Keys.

Piper's smile disappeared again. Seemed she had smiles for everyone but him. What had he been thinking? Flying all the way to France!

She hadn't answered his question. He decided to wish her well and get out of there as fast as he could. Then a tall, lanky teenager ambushed his escape. "Neil!" The kid enveloped him in a quick hard hug.

It was Nandan. What the— They weren't supposed to know each other. Why hadn't he even once thought about her brother blowing his cover? He pretended confusion. "Do I know—"

"It's okay." Nandan stepped back but kept a hand on Neil's shoulder. His grin was huge in his thin face. "My sister knows." His English was heavily accented but clear.

Neil glanced at Piper. She knew? The look in her eyes was unmistakable. Gratitude.

But he didn't want her gratitude.

Nandan was oblivious to Neil's disgruntled state. He leaned in. "Though we cannot announce it, you are our guest of honor. I wanted to thank you in person, so..." He dropped the hand clasping Neil's shoulder and extended his right hand. "Thank you. My heart has no words."

Neil took Nandan's hand and the kid pumped it vigorously. The boy was still recovering from his ordeal, but he'd definitely filled out. His grip was strong and his eyes sparkled with happiness.

He wished he could say the same for Piper right now. She had tears glistening in her eyes. His gut twisted. He didn't want her to be upset. He changed his mind. He'd take gratitude.

She hugged Nandan. "I need to speak with Neil privately, Nan. Will you excuse us for a few minutes?"

"How you Americans say? No problem." The boy gave Neil the thumbs-up sign and then kissed his sister's cheek and wove into the crowd.

Neil snagged a drink off a passing tray. He didn't care what it was; he gulped it down.

She faced him, hands clasped tightly in front of her. "I wanted to thank you, also."

"No need." He tugged at the collar of his starched shirt.

"But I wish you had told me what you planned. What if you'd been caught? Or killed? I'd have never known."

"Exactly."

"Oh, Neil."

Oh, Neil—what? Oh, Neil, I hate you? Oh, Neil, I forgive you?

Glancing around her, she took his hand and led him out of the ballroom to the bottom of the wide winding staircase.

Dress swishing, she spoke as they walked. "Nandan

told me everything. How you carried him." She lowered her head but not before he saw the tear tracks on her cheeks.

"Aw, sweetheart, don't cry." He reached up to wipe the corner of her eye and caressed her cheek. "Everything turned out fine."

"Nandan said you were hurt. Are you okay now?"

"It was nothing. I told you. It's all good."

"Good? Neil, you gave up being a SEAL! The one thing you loved. I can't believe you did that."

"I was getting out anyway. Believe me—"

"Because you never lie?"

"I didn't lie to you. I *was* going on a mission."

She pursed her lips and folded her arms across her chest.

Neil blinked. "All right, so I sort of lied."

One dark brow arched. "And you conveniently never mentioned having a wife."

Okay, this was not how he'd seen this night going. "I never mentioned her because as far as I was concerned, I was divorced. I didn't want to think about her when I was with you. Why am I explaining myself to you?" He turned to head back into the ballroom. He'd call a cab and… He stopped. Leave Piper out here alone? Unprotected? He spun back around. "Where is Jim anyway?"

"I stopped getting the threatening letters, so I let him go."

"You what?"

She shrugged. "I figured since I wasn't seeing you anymore, the creep got what he wanted."

No choice now. He was going to have to tell her. "My ex is the one who sent you the letters."

"What?" Piper stood there, blinking. "Why?"

Neil heaved a sigh and closed his eyes. "Lyndsey thought she could postpone the divorce. She cooked up the scheme because her boss kept asking her to use me to influence my father."

Piper's cute little nose crinkled. "What does your father have to do with your ex-wife?"

Neil winced. "You know he's a senator, right? Lyndsey's a lobbyist for one of his biggest donors. Patrick Barrow is the master of the quid pro quo. The divorce makes him look bad. It's an election year. You do the math."

"And were you ever going to tell me this?"

"They're ready for you, Piper," Ragi called from the ballroom doorway.

Piper hesitated. "Thank you, Ragi." She turned hurt and confused eyes on him. "I have to go."

As she stepped past him, he caught her hand. "I'm sorry. I should've told you."

While Piper climbed the steps to the dais with Francois Giroux, Neil slipped into the crowd and snagged another drink from a passing waiter. His gut twisted. The look in her eyes. She thought he was a liar. Maybe she even thought that he'd had something to do with the letters.

The band played a brief fanfare and the room grew silent as all eyes turned to the Frenchman.

"*Mesdames et messieurs*, ladies and gentlemen," Francois spoke into the mike. "*Bienvenue*. Welcome.

I am your host, Monsieur Giroux, and tonight we are here to raise money for Nandan's House, a home for the impoverished children of Delhi."

Applause broke out, and Francois gestured for Piper to step forward. "This children's charity is the dream of international supermodel Piper."

Piper stepped up to the mike. "*Bon soir.* Thank you for coming." She scanned the crowd, her expression serious. "There are many homeless families in India. Homeless children in particular are at risk, sometimes subject to illness, abuse, forced labor and even abduction."

Neil wondered if anyone else noticed how her hands gripped the mike stand so tightly.

Piper continued, "Giving children a home, a place where they know they will be safe, and from which they can go on to have a chance at a healthy and positive future, will make a great deal of difference to many. It may even save lives. Nandan's House is one such point of refuge, a sanctuary, a safe haven. I have promised to make it so, but I cannot do it alone. My dear friends, together we *can* make a difference. So tonight, I beg of you, be generous."

More applause. Piper flashed her internationally known smile. Francois announced that there would now be dancing, and refreshments were being served in the next room. Then he kissed the back of Piper's hand and kept hold of it as he helped her down the steps.

The orchestra started up again and the middle of the room cleared as a few couples began dancing.

Neil watched Piper mix into the throng of gowns

and tuxes, working the room. Greeting people, kissing cheeks, touching arms.

Neil was going to leave. But he wanted to talk to security first. And he would at least tell her goodbye. He hadn't gotten that chance the last time. He elbowed his way through the crowd until he reached her.

She stopped talking the moment she saw him and included him into the circle of people with whom she'd been speaking. "Neil, this is Cassandra Moray, my friend and Desiree's Desire model. Cass, *this* is Neil."

The tall, gorgeous black woman's eyes widened. "*The* Neil? Who cost you the endorsement contract with Modelle?"

"Cass!" Piper hissed.

Neil felt sucker punched. "You lost a contract because of me?"

"Dance with me," Piper said a little too brightly as she gripped his arm and pulled him to the dance floor. She glanced behind her and caught the eye of the conductor, who immediately stopped the orchestra to change songs.

Neil took her right hand in his, put his other hand at the small of her back and swept her into a slow box step. Then he recognized the song. "Key Largo." His throat tightened. "I've really messed up your life, haven't I?"

She looked up at him. "You gave me back my brother. I'd give up a thousand endorsements for that."

The emotion in her voice made his chest ache. He owed her the truth. "I suppose it was from some vestige of loyalty to Lyndsey that I didn't tell you about her sending the letters. If you'd pressed charges, she could've ended up in prison. I've since heard that she's had a breakdown and is finally getting some help."

"It doesn't matter." Piper's intense gaze set his pulse to racing. She moved her hand from his shoulder to the back of his neck and threaded her fingers through his hair. "You let your hair grow longer."

Neil closed his eyes, reveling in her touch. His breathing quickened. How he wanted this woman. As they swayed back and forth, he moved his palm up over the soft skin of her back.

"You are my hero, you know." Piper referenced a line of the lyrics.

He resisted the urge to call her his leading lady. If this was back to being just about gratitude, he didn't want it. But then, why had she ordered that song? Against his better judgment, he pulled her closer. Brushed his lips against her temple and caught a whiff of her exotic scent. "I'm just a guy, Piper."

"Could we have it all, do you think?" Piper slid her other arm around his back.

What was she really asking? Did she want to take up where they'd left off? Even if she did, he didn't think he could survive another failed relationship. "I don't know." He honestly didn't. "Your gala seems to be a big success."

She leaned back, stared into his eyes. "Are you surprised?"

"Not a bit. I never believed you were the bad girl everyone said you were."

"Oh, I don't know. I can be bad when I want to be." She lifted her chin and bit his earlobe.

He missed a step and stumbled over his own feet.

"Would you like to see what I'm *not* wearing under this dress?"

That was it. He stopped dancing. "Piper. What is it we're doing here?"

"Come with me." She took his hand and led him off the dance floor.

19

IGNORING HER RACING HEART, Piper led Neil out through a set of French doors to the stone balcony overlooking the Mediterranean. She wandered over to the marble balustrade and leaned against it, looking out at the moonlit night. A perfect night for romance.

If only Neil wanted her as she wanted him.

Stepping up beside her, he braced his forearms on the railing. She caught the scent of his musky cologne on the breeze.

To have him so close and yet have this chasm between them… It hurt. But he'd flown all the way here from America. That had to mean something. The song hadn't had the effect she'd hoped it would. Maybe there was too much between them to make a go of it. But she wasn't giving up without a fight.

She glanced over at him. He looked magnificent in his tux. Although she preferred him in cargo shorts and a T-shirt. He simply wasn't a tuxedo kind of guy.

hat was what she was counting on. "Let's go down to the garden."

Nervous. Scared. Hopeful. Piper clutched her skirt and lifted the hem so that she had little trouble as she descended the stairs that wound down to a terraced, manicured garden. Glancing back to make sure he was following her, she made her way to the fountain in the center of the circular garden. The fountain was so big she'd once climbed in and frolicked around. She'd been tipsy then. And silly.

But tonight, as he stopped beside her, she very deliberately dipped her hand into the water and splashed him.

It soaked the front of his suit. "Hey, what's the…?"

Oh, the look on his face! It was the last thing he'd expected. Laughing mischievously, she spun on her heels and rushed down the path.

"You little— Come back here!" He chased her, but it was dark, and she had the advantage of knowing where she was going. Laughing as he called out, threatening to get her, she darted off the path and raced up a hill toward the marble gazebo. As she reached it, he grabbed her around the waist and lifted her off her feet. She shrieked and he spun her around to face him. She was breathless, but he barely seemed winded. He let her slowly slide down his body. The water on his suit was cold, but his chest beneath was hot.

With a whimper she wound her arms around his neck and kissed him. Kisses that revealed to him everything stored in her heart.

He groaned, sweeping his tongue in to taste her.

She pushed him backward, and when he plopped

onto a bench, she straddled his lap, desperately hiking up her skirt. His lips left kisses from along her shoulder to the tops of her breasts. Oh, the feel of his mouth on her bare skin. He cupped her breasts, caressed them while she tugged at his bow tie and slid it off.

"Piper." He voice was strained, yearning with passion. Unzipping her gown, he eased the bodice lower, baring her nipples.

"I've missed you so, Neil." Tearing his suit coat off his shoulders, she got to work unbuttoning his shirt. She needed his warm skin against hers, needed to be as close to him as possible.

He leaned back and fumbled with the zipper on his trousers; still, he was quick to free his erection, and then she was sinking onto him.

It was her turn to groan, and for a long moment neither of them moved as his mouth found hers again. For months she'd longed for this—this oneness with him. Only Neil.

She was where she'd longed to be. In his arms, his hard length inside her, his sensuous lips playing over hers. She began to rock, and he gripped her hips and encouraged her with sighs and whispers at her ear. "Yes," she murmured in reply.

His mouth worshipped hers. She'd never felt so loved, so desired. And when he came she could feel it in every way and see it, too, in the way he tilted his head back and the veins in his neck stood out. Watching him come took her over the edge of bliss and she cried his name, not caring who saw or heard.

Then he was placing gentle kisses on her nose and

ıeeks and temples and forehead until she slumped against him, happy and sated.

His fingers made lazy curlicues across her back, down her spine, inside her loosened dress.

As they sat together like that for a short while, the only sounds were their breathing and the chirping of night insects.

At last, she lifted her head from his shoulder, smiling, drawing in a deep, deep breath. "I love you."

He frowned and shifted beneath her.

Her smile and happiness vanished in a puff of embarrassment. She clutched her gown to her breasts and scrambled off his lap.

"Piper, I—"

"Don't." She turned her back and struggled to get the stupid zipper up. Behind her, she heard the rustle of his trousers as he stood and then gasped.

She twisted to see that his right knee had buckled.

"You're hurt!" she exclaimed.

"I'm fine." But when he started to move, he limped.

She knelt and placed a palm on the knee he was favoring. She wanted to kiss it and make it better. She wanted to take care of him, as he'd taken care of her. She wanted a lifetime of them taking care of each other.

"Piper, it's fine." He removed her hand and she straightened.

Without limping, he retrieved his coat and tie from where they'd fallen behind the bench.

"Is that why you're…" She waved a hand, incapable of saying the words *rejecting me*.

"No." He faced her. "I'm not that self-sacrificing. And I'm not going to lie to you anymore."

"I see." A terrible hurt seized her chest and settled in. "I better get back. Francois will—"

"Piper, let me explain."

"No, no. I get it. Don't need to be hit over the head when a simple no will suffice." She picked up her skirt to walk down the hill easier.

Neil grasped her shoulders from behind. "Hold on a second. And let. Me. Explain."

If she struggled, she'd cry. And if she cried she'd smear her mascara. She could return to the party with her hair a little mussed, but she bloody well wasn't going back there with mascara running down her cheeks. "I'm listening."

"Okay." Drawing a deep breath, he loosened his hold on her shoulders but he didn't let her go. "About five years ago I was working at the Pentagon and fell in love with an air force pilot. However, she was in love with someone else. Looking back on it, I think my eventual marriage to Lyndsey was more about Alex's rejection than it was about wanting Lindsay."

Piper closed her eyes. It was like a stab in the heart to hear him admit that he'd loved someone else.

"I've known Lyndsey since I was a kid. Her parents were friends with my parents at the club. She and I were the same age, and we both liked chess and horseback riding. I think we were both alone a lot." He shrugged. "We were friends."

Piper shivered.

"Here." He left her briefly, then returned to drape

his coat over her shoulders. Sliding his arms around her waist, he drew her against him. Her back was pressed to his chest, and she covered his hands with hers.

"Over the years I'd see Lyndsey occasionally at her parents' annual holiday party. A few years ago, I'd just turned thirty, and we were both standing around miserable." He cleared his throat. "This next part is hard to admit."

Piper waited.

"I was lonely. I'd convinced myself that love just wasn't going to happen for me. And I wanted a family."

She felt him shrug.

"Lyndsey and I had a lot in common. We had similar life goals. At least, I thought we did. Even after the blinders came off about six months in, I thought I could make it work."

He sighed. "I was gone often—that's the life of a SEAL—so it was easy to make excuses for the gulf I felt growing between us. Lyndsey works insane hours. I knew something wasn't right, but even then, I never suspected—"

Piper wanted to turn around, but she sensed this was easier for him to do without facing her. She squeezed his hands encouragingly.

"I'd been overseas on an op for six months. When I got stateside I headed straight home after debriefing. It was the middle of the night, so I sneaked into the bedroom without turning on the lights. Thought maybe I'd try to talk to her about starting over. I pulled back the sheet to crawl into bed." He blew out a harsh breath. "And my leg hit another man's leg."

"No..." Piper did turn into him then and caressed his cheek, but he wouldn't meet her gaze.

"You know what she said? She said she was sorry I'd had to find out that way, but she couldn't really be expected to be faithful to me when I was gone so much." He grimaced. "The sad thing is, I wasn't even that mad. I was more embarrassed than anything else."

Piper reached up and kissed the corner of his mouth. "You deserve better, Neil. You deserve to be loved."

He was silent a long time, and then he pierced her with a meaningful look. "You're right. I won't settle for less next time."

She pulled away, stepping back. "So you doubt my love? You think I'm like Lyndsey?"

"No. Just...young. Piper, you're so young. I'm what? A decade or so older than you? At your age you barely know what you want."

Fury smoldered and burned off the hurt that had buried into her chest. "That's rather insulting. You're the one who said I'd done a lot of living in my twenty-three years. I run my own company, manage a charity foundation. That's not something most people my age do."

"And that's another thing," he continued as if she hadn't spoken. "You have a whole life I could never be a part of, even if I wanted to, which I don't."

She couldn't believe him, wouldn't believe him. "You're just a coward. You've been hurt and betrayed and so you're afraid it will happen again. Well, welcome to life, Neil, where bad things happen and we have to get on with it."

He clasped her shoulders, stared into her eyes. "Can

you honestly see me jetting around with your millionaire friends? I want a family, Piper. Soon. Are you ready to settle down in a bungalow in Florida and raise a couple of kids with me?"

She shook him off. "Life doesn't have to be either or." She wanted to explain, but what would it change? She let out a resigned breath. "Be happy, Neil. You deserve everything good."

Before she made more of a fool of herself than she already had, she turned and marched down the steps of the gazebo and along the grassy hillside. It hadn't seemed so steep running up. But she hadn't been blinded by tears then. And she wasn't hearing the sound of a man chasing after her, either. Her face crumpled then and she couldn't stop crying.

She didn't want anyone to see her, especially not in this state. But there were good people here she needed to thank for coming. Her pity party could wait.

However, there was no going back into Francois's ballroom until she cleaned up. She changed direction and headed for the mansion's side entrance. There was a pool house with a restroom where she could repair her makeup and hair.

A man stepped into her path. Neil!

She looked up.

Before she could scream, a hand clamped over her mouth.

It wasn't Neil.

20

NEIL HAD LET her go.

When what he had really wanted to do, more than anything, was to run after her.

But he knew he was right. She'd think she loved him for a while at least, and then she'd meet someone else. A guy from her high-profile world, no doubt.

He buttoned his shirt and tucked it into his pants, slid the bow tie around the collar but left it untied and shrugged into his damp coat. He smiled. Mischievous imp, splashing him like that.

She was like no one else he knew. Strong, passionate, wicked...loving. How was a man supposed to think straight after having her in his arms, making love, hearing those three precious words? He hadn't meant to let things go that far, though. She probably believed he'd gotten what he wanted from her. Again.

Couldn't she understand why they were doomed to fail?

He wanted kids, and sometime before he had to at-end their high school graduations using a walker. She wouldn't want to have kids anytime soon. Couldn't exactly model lingerie with a big pregnant belly. Although that arousing, wonderful image of Piper was now permanently etched on his brain.

Back to the point, Barrow.

Him and Piper. Not working. Somebody had to be the sensible one. The reasons it wouldn't work far outweighed the reasons it could. Although…

Was he being a coward? Making excuses so he wouldn't get hurt again? Was it just about trust?

She'd trusted him tonight with her heart. Even after the whole debacle with Lyndsey. That couldn't have been easy.

But if this thing failed with Piper, then that was his third strike. She was right. He was protecting his heart. Three strikes and he'd be out. Likely, he'd be unable to recover. And not because it would be failure number three, but because that was how much he loved her.

So it was better to lose her now?

To hell with getting his heart shattered. If all they had was a year or two, then he'd deal with that when it happened. He was a class-one moron to let her go.

Cursing, he jumped off the gazebo and hit the grass running. His knee screamed in agony, but he refused to register the pain. He'd ice it later.

He could barely see her ahead of him, but he raced on. She'd already made it to the path with the rose trellis. He watched as she crossed abruptly to the left when she reached the fountain instead of continuing straight toward the main steps.

Suddenly she disappeared behind a thick hedge. Where was she going? He jogged after her, cutting through the landscaped flowerbeds. He turned the corner and—

Neil tore down the path, watching helplessly as Piper struggled to get out of some guy's hold. She managed to pull away, but he still had a grip on her arms and was shaking her.

Red-hot fury overtook Neil.

Closing in on them, he reared back and flung his fist at the thug's jaw. He heard a satisfying crack and Piper's attacker dropped to the ground. The guy was out for the count.

Neil swung Piper into his arms. "Are you all right?" She clung to him, shivering and gulping deep breaths. Pain shot up his arm and he carefully wagged his hand, pretty sure he'd broken it. "Who was that guy?"

"I don't know. I've never met him. He was insane, saying I'd invited him and that he knew I loved him."

"I never should have let you go off alone."

She stiffened and shrugged out of his arms. "This isn't your fault."

Neil closed his eyes briefly. "You need a bodyguard, Piper. You're a world-famous person."

"Fine. I'll hire someone. Thank you for—that." She waved in the direction of the unconscious assailant. She tried to move away, but Neil caught her elbow with his good hand. "Wait."

She glanced up at him. Conflicting emotions were apparent in her face. "What?"

She was shaken. Disheveled. It didn't seem like the

time to tell her. And tell her what exactly? That he'd changed his mind? That just the thought of living without her had made him see that he wanted to try, to risk… everything.

Maybe she wouldn't believe him now. She'd think he was merely trying to protect her. After she had a few moments to put herself together, then he'd tell her.

"You're not going anywhere alone," he replied.

She frowned. "Fine."

"And I need to get someone out here to arrest this creep."

"Oh, right. I'll tell Francois."

She rubbed her forehead, then looked toward the mansion and headed back the way they'd come.

He walked beside her, his mind struggling with how to say what he wanted to say.

"You're limping. Oh, and your hand!" She'd stopped in her tracks and was now staring at him, shocked.

He hadn't realized he'd allowed himself to limp. And he was cradling his hand against his chest. "It needs some ice."

"Ice! It's swollen to twice its normal size. We're going to the hospital."

Before she could set off, he stepped closer to her. "Piper."

"Don't argue with me. You're going to have a doctor look at your hand. And what's wrong with your leg anyway—"

He kissed her, this time with his good hand holding the back of her head. "I love you, too," he murmured against her lips.

She stilled beneath his touch, flattened her hands on his chest and shoved. He staggered back. "*Now* you tell me this? Now?"

"You don't believe me." He reached out to catch her, but she employed evasive maneuvers, spinning and hiking up her skirt to leave. "You think this attack just made me scared."

"Of course not. I know you love me. I only wish you'd—"

"Wait. You know?"

"Neil." She gave him an exasperated look. "A man doesn't quit a job he loves, sneak into enemy territory on his own and risk his life to save the brother of someone he *doesn't* love." She gently covered his swollen hand. "We'll talk later, now, please, let's get you to a doctor?"

"No." His hand was throbbing, but it could wait. "I don't want to make this any worse than I already have." He caressed her cheek. "I do love you, Piper. I want to spend my life with you. I don't know how it will work, but I'll do whatever it takes to *make* it work."

She cradled his face between her palms. "That's exactly why it will work, Neil. Because we both want it to." She pressed a tender, loving kiss to his mouth. "I know you think I'm this irresponsible bad girl, but I'm not that person anymore."

"Yeah, about that. I kind of like it when you're bad."

She smiled. "You do?"

He touched his forehead to hers and grinned.

"Neil?"

"Hmm?"

"We probably ought to call someone about—" She nodded in the direction of the still unconscious assailant. "Him."

Neil scowled, still furious that she could've been hurt or worse. "And you need to hire a bodyguard."

She beamed wickedly. "It just so happens I know a guy."

* * * * *

Don't miss author Jillian Burns's next FEVER *title coming this fall from Harlequin Blaze!*

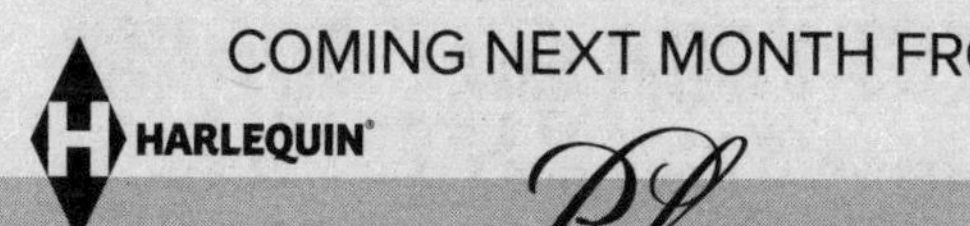

Available June 16, 2015

#851 THUNDERSTRUCK

Thunder Mountain Brotherhood

by Vicki Lewis Thompson

Cowboy-turned-contractor Damon Harrison comes home to Thunder Mountain to help with a building project. But when he meets the carpenter Philomena Turner, they have so much spark they might just burn down the bunkhouse.

#852 IN TOO DEEP

SEALs of Fortune

by Kira Sinclair

Ex-SEAL Knox McLemore needs to prove the shipwreck they found is really the *Chimera*, but tightly buttoned nautical archaeologist Avery Walsh has her own agenda. And he's determined to uncover what she's hiding...one button at a time!

#853 HOT IN THE CITY

by Samantha Hunter

Math whiz Della Clark wants to swap equations for a wild fling when she meets flirty hunk Gabe Ross. Until Gabe's true identity throws their chance for a happy-ever-after into dire jeopardy.

#854 BEST MAN...WITH BENEFITS

The Wrong Bed

by Nancy Warren

From a wedding to a bedding! Somehow maid of honor Lauren Sanger wound up between the sheets with sexy—but irritating!—best man Jackson Monaghan. Pure sexual bliss...but will their secret relationship last?

SPECIAL EXCERPT FROM

Blaze

Nautical archaeologist Avery Walsh knows former navy SEAL Knox McLemore will hate her when he learns the truth. But she can't resist the heat between them!

Read on for a sneak preview of
IN TOO DEEP,
a ***SEALS OF FORTUNE*** *novel by* Kira Sinclair.

"Keep looking at me that way and we're going to do something we'll both regret."

Avery jerked her gaze from Knox's bare chest to his eyes. "How am I looking at you?"

"Like you want to run that gorgeous mouth all over me."

"Hmm…maybe I do." She could hear her own words, a little slow, a little slurred.

"You're drunk, Doc."

Flopping back onto the sand, Avery propped her head against Knox's thigh.

She stared up at him, his head haloed by the black sky and twinkling stars. They both seemed so far away—Knox and the heavens.

"I've never gotten drunk and made bad decisions before," she said. "Was hoping we could make one together."

He made a sound, a cross between a laugh, a wheeze and a groan. "What kind of bad decision did you have in mind?"

"Oh, you know, giving in to the sexual tension that's been clawing at us since the day we met. But I guess you're not drunk enough yet to want me."

HBEXP0615

ıst me when I say I don't have to be drunk to want ıvery."

ne made a scoffing sound. "You don't even like me."

Slowly, Knox smoothed his hand across her face, ıngers gliding from cheekbone to forehead to chin.

"I like you just fine, Doc," he whispered, his voice gruff and smoky. The words spilled across her skin like warm honey.

He growled low in his throat. His palm landed on her belly, spreading wide and applying the slightest pressure. "I'm fighting to do the right thing."

"What if I don't want you to do the right thing?"

She felt the tremor in his hand, the commanding force weighing her down. If he stopped touching her she might float off into the night and never find her way back.

"I don't take advantage of women who are inebriated." His words were harsh, but his eyes glowed as they stared down at her. Devoured her.

Never in her life had she felt so…desired. And she wanted that. Wanted him.

"Please."

Avery was certain that in the morning she'd hate herself for that single word and how close she sounded to ·egging. But right now, she didn't care.

"Please," she whispered again, just to make sure he ·new she meant it.

HBEXP0615